Nathan Robinson

Ketchup on Everything

Snake BITE Publishing

Text copyright © 2014 Nathan Robinson

All Rights Reserved

Published by Snakebite Horror

www.snakebitehorror.co.uk

Front cover design by Kay Vincent/Ketchup on Everything copyright 2014

www.ketchuponeverything.co.uk

All Rights Reserved.

"Find what you love and let it kill you"

Attributed to Kinky Friedman

To Catherine

Happy reading!

Much Love

Nathan Robinson

INTRODUCTION

Around four years back, when I was just new to the review game, I created a section on Snakebite Horror dedicated to showcasing the talent of new writers. This is where I met Nathan Robinson. Nathan was starting out on the writing business and had appeared in a few anthologies but he decided to send a story in to our then VERY little website. Top of the Heap was brilliant! It showcased what is great about new up and coming horror writers here in the UK. From there on Nathan and I started talking. I helped push his stories and he did the occasional book review for the site and then around two years ago Nathan became Snakebite Horror's head of fiction reviews.

From there Nathan released some great books, Starers being one of his huge hits, and that's when a copy of this book landed on my desk and the book which I thought was good enough to launch the newest Snakebite Horror venture, Snakebite Publishing.

'Ketchup on Everything' may only be a short one, but what Nathan puts in to these pages are more emotional than a lot of Indie Horror writers can do. This is probably one of the best novellas I have read in a LONG time, so sit back and get ready to enjoy an emotional tale of loss and obsession with a nice little twist.

Mark Goddard-Snakebite Horror Editor
www.snakebitehorror.co.uk

Ketchup on Everything

Ketchup on Everything

Ketchup on Everything

The sign said *Sheardown's Steak House and Diner*, inscribed in a faux Western frontier style script and complete with unlit bullet holes. The dust-coated motor home trundled into the potholed car park with a scrape of rubber on rock. The cabin jostled over the uneven surface until it found its place beneath an oak tree, stopping between a beaten up Volvo and a freshly waxed Range Rover. The driver turned off the lights, silencing the blues show that poured from the speakers with a twist of the volume button, then killed the engine. He listened to the seething clicks of mechanical chambers and oily catacombs that hissed along with the insectile population of the nearby field of fragrant rapeseed. It was time to stop; it was approaching that awkward time of day when twilight denied him the finer details of the road and he didn't like driving in the dark.

Elliott Tather leant forward and looked out at the diner, his back grateful as it popped out the tension of sitting in the driver's seat for far too long. He could have parked closer, but he felt an aching need to stretch his legs. He'd been barrelling down the Great North Road all day, pulling up at every service station and supermarket he came across. He must have spoken to a hundred people in the past twelve hours. Tomorrow he planned to cut through Norfolk and cover the southern part of the east coast of England, doing much the same again.

But that was the tedium for tomorrow.

Tather cracked his jaw, then his knuckles; one to ten in gratifying succession. He looked at the prematurely old man in the rear view mirror. It wasn't him. He was a good few years off fifty but the grey had singed the brown into submission, making him look ten years older.

Where had this old man come from?

He blinked his watery blues, which always seemed on the edge of tears for various reasons.

'Reckon this'll do,' he said, considering the low laying diner with a tired squint. 'I only want a coffee, flask is empty and I don't reckon we'll ever make the coast on caffeine fumes alone.' Tather turned to his wife, Susannah, who sat at peace in the middle seat beside him, quiet as usual. He imagined an answer for her.

'Maybe even a slice of cheesecake. I think I've earned it.' Tather unbuckled himself, and then unfolded his spindly form from the cab, onto the gravel, his back popping involuntarily this time. He turned to his wife, hands on hips, leaning back to press the tension from the curve of his spine.

'Ouch!' He winced as the pressure flew free from his lower back. 'That's better. You gonna come along darling?'

Susannah remained silent and still as usual. Elliott Tather smiled to himself and sighed.

'No worries, you get your head down if you want. I won't be long.' He closed the door to the motor home, locked it and headed across the car park towards the diner, absentmindedly kicking loose stones into the bushes as he went. One

Ketchup on Everything

pinged off the fuel tank of a parked furniture lorry.

Looking skyward, the fat, blind eye of the moon peeked from behind a passing spectre-like cloud, his only witness on this balmy evening. The cloud passed, and the moon was free to float, bright and beaming, unchallenged by the weather.

The diner was a squat building constructed of chrome panelling and neon strip lights along the rim of the roof to give it that authentic Americana diner feel that the English seemed to find so delightfully kitsch. Tather had to walk the entire length of it to get to the main door. Inside he could make out red and blue leather booths, only two of which were occupied; a lorry driver in a dark blue Dickies work shirt mopping the grease from his face with a napkin and a father joking around with his son and daughter. Both groups looked content and brimming full of starch and sugar.

In the porch area he could sense greasy egg, the burn of bacon and the faint tang of bleach seeping into the night air. Good grub and cleanliness were decent and comforting smells in any eating establishment.

Tather entered the diner and a young Elvis harped out a ghostly version of *Blue Moon*, which, despite the close heat of the August night, sent shivers down his back and arms. Billie Holiday's version had been his first dance at his wedding to Susannah. Regardless of the eerie soundtrack he continued onwards into the den of retro memorabilia.

Old 45 sleeves made up a collage of faces, colours and band names on the wall surrounding the serving hatch to his right. The kitchen beyond was well lit but devoid of the usual human noise and busyness. Along the walls were pictures of Hollywood greats. On the wall next to him, Tather noticed in a strip of three, top, middle, bottom; Dean Martin with a drunken grin slurred across his face, the wayward tumbler in his hand testament to this, James Dean, smoking a moody cigarette whilst leaning on a stoic horse and bizarrely, Cliff Richard dressed head to toe in polyester, in a pose that managed to harness everything about 80's nostalgia.

Fire the interior designer, was Elliott's first thought.

'We've stopped doing food,' said the pleasant-faced waitress emerging from a doorway behind the counter. Her hair was tied up and back. She wrangled a few loose strands in place behind her ear before meeting his gaze with earnest green eyes.

'Chef's gone home.' She wiped her hands on a dish towel and tossed it beside the till. She had a slight air of glamour about her; maybe she'd modelled in her youth and looked after herself well with plenty of water and early nights. But with age maybe the work had dried up and she'd taken the only job she was qualified for. Tather imagined a husband trading her in for a younger, faster model and all the pain she felt, the bitter anguish and tear soaked pillows. Inside, he shrugged at his own speculation. It was nice to think about other people's problems for a change, even if they only existed in his own exploratory imagination.

She smiled whilst she waited for his response. But from the way the grin struck up her cheeks and defined her dimples too proud, Elliott could see she was tired and just wanted to finish up for the night. It was false and part of the job. It did nothing to convince him of true joy. Maybe the boss had told her to always smile at the customers; no matter how much of a crappy day you were having. She wanted him to turn and leave, that's what the smile said. That was how he read it. For a moment he considered it. He didn't want to be any trouble, but his stomach growled otherwise. He needed to be selfish and furnish himself with some form of sustenance and a brief moment of human contact away from the slog of the road, no matter how sparse. He'd been talking back to the radio all day; he needed a face and eyes to look back at him to keep the unending loneliness at bay. Even for a few minutes, *that would do.*

He blinked out his fugue, slightly ashamed that his wonder at her beauty had caused him to stop dumb in his tracks.

At the far end of the diner, the Dickies-shirted lorry driver drained his beer, pulled his bulbous gut out from under the table and walked the length of the diner with a lumbering strut. He passed Tather, giving him a kind regard with a gentlemanly nod, then the knight of the road was off and into the pleasant mooned night.

Tather walked up to the counter. 'I'd just like a coffee if that's okay?'

'Sure. Cook's had to shoot early with a tummy bug, so unless you want a toasted sandwich or soup, a hot drink is all you're getting,' the waitress said with another wry and tired smile. He didn't ask for much, and that was what he was getting.

Outside the furniture lorry revved up and pulled out of the gravel car park, barrelling into the depths of the darkening day.

'A black coffee's fine.'

The waitress turned to the coffee machine with a repetitive swish and placed a cup beneath the spout. The machine made frothing and bubbling noises whilst the black liquid spat out into the cup. Tather cast his hungering gaze over the chiller cabinet. A solitary slice of pie sat on a crumb scattered plate.

'What pie is that?'

The waitress turned and placed the full, steaming cup on the counter. Tather caught sight of her name tag; **Simone**.

'Apple and blackberry. Home-made,' Simone said with a cheery brightening of her eyes. Tather cracked a half smile that almost hurt.

'Did you make it?'

'Ha. No. I just serve the food. Denise is the dessert queen. We get the blackberries from a bramble bush in the field out back. The apples come from an orchard about two miles away. It's local with a low carbon footprint. You want the last slice?'

'I believe I will. My wife used to make me this back in the day. Now I have to watch the calories.'

'Pah, there's nothing on you. You could do with fattening up if anything!' Simone smiled.

'I like the clothes I've got. They make me look younger than I am.'

'Younger? I bet you've only just hit forty?' She teased.

'Huh, are you trying to flatter me? I'm well over forty. I've just lived.'

'Haven't we all?'

Elliott watched as Simone leant into the chiller cabinet and carefully retrieved the last piece of pie on a cake slice. Her white cotton shirt hung low revealing two fine bumps of womanly curves. Feeling embarrassed, Elliott turned his gaze to the menu board. Simone was about his age, and was still in fine form, but he wanted to keep the conversation on food and service. For a brief moment he imagined asking Simone about herself, maybe even trying to "*chat her up*".

He smiled and imagined the fallout.

How would a nice lady like her put up with the mess his life had become? Maybe she'd be sympathetic and let him talk about it. Maybe she could be the one to help him move on, perhaps even be the start of a new chapter in his life.

Maybe she had her own problems.

Beside the till was a stack of clean, white plates. She placed the pie on the top plate then placed it onto the counter. Tather started fumbling in his pockets for change. Simone made no effort to ring it in on the till.

'What's the damage?'

'No charge,' Simone said, lowering her tone.

'What?'

'No charge. I've already banked up and I can't be bothered to open the till again. I was about five minutes from throwing that last slice of two day old pie away when you walked in. And a coffee is just a coffee. Consider yourself our lucky customer of the day.'

'That's very kind of you. You can't beat free pie.' Tather forgave her fake smile. Clearly she had a kindly heart that betrayed her weary nature.

A stern-faced woman stepped out from the ladies toilet. The family sat in the booth stood up to greet her. The kids ran out excitedly, riding on a wave of sugar. The father smiled in the wry way humans do when they want to acknowledge your existence but without the need for conversation. The wife made no effort to engage Simone or Elliott as she left.

'Thank you for coming,' Simone called after them.

The door clicked shut behind the family and Elvis got into the final verse of Blue Moon.

'You sure about the charge?'

'Listen, I've tilled up, I just want to get this place cleaned up and go home. It's just nice to have someone around. Some nights you get weirdo truckers hitting on you. The other night we had a van with blacked out windows parked in the car park all night. I don't need that. I know they're lonely and everything, but I'm sure they've got wives at home.'

'How do you know I'm not some weirdo trucker?'

'I saw your motor home, plus you're married,' Simone stroked her ring finger, and then pointed to the band on Tather's hand. 'Plus I heard you talking to someone inside the camper when I went to take the rubbish out back. I'm guessing your wife is asleep. You're retired, right? Travelling around the country seeing the sights?'

Tather half smiled at the assumption. He looked out to his motor home; he couldn't see it from inside the diner. The Range Rover that he'd parked next to reversed then ambled out of the car park with the family inside. Tather wished that they got home safe and well and lived long and happy lives.

'You're like Sherlock Holmes with those astute deductions. You guess right; wifey's asleep in the camper. I took early retirement, but I'm much younger than I look. I've just had one of those lives.'

Simone gave a forgiving smile. 'Same here.'

A moment of mutual appreciation passed between them. Someone needed to say something. It was him. He held his hands up to protest his innocence.

'Listen, I just want a coffee. I'm not a weirdo. But I'll stick around until you're done if you want. The least I can do for free pie.'

'I'd appreciate it.' Simone reached into the cutlery tray and placed a spoon on the plate next to the pie.

'Am I okay to make camp in the car park for the night? I didn't see any signs saying not.'

'Free pie and you want a bed for the night? You're pushing it mister!' she jested. 'Yeah it should be fine, just try and make sure you're gone before six. Herbert the owner opens up in the morning and he might have a few harsh words for you. He's best avoided. Even on his good days.'

'Cheers, thank you. I hoped to make the coast before nightfall but we hit a bit of city traffic on the ring road. Now I just want to sleep.' Tather retrieved a few coins from his pocket and dropped them in the British Heart Foundation charity box that sat forlornly on the counter. Simone gave a smile that reflected his cares.

'I'll be shutting shop in about fifteen minutes, just so you know.' Simone leant into the chiller cabinet and picked up the empty pie platter and headed back into the kitchen to wash up.

Tather picked up the plate that held his apple and blackberry pie and his black coffee then headed to the far end of the diner where a cosy booth was tucked in around the corner. The rest of the booths had detritus from meals and spills from coffee, coke and milkshakes. The end booth was clean and it had a view of the television, which displayed rolling misery on low volume.

Atlantic Tsunami warning...

Banks suggest higher deposits on mortgages...

Forty dead in Kabul blast...

Doom, gloom, boom. The news never seemed to change, Tather had gotten used to bad news. Once you found yourself in a bad news bubble, it was hard to tell when it'd burst, if at all. When did bad luck end and normal luck start up again, if at all?

Tather didn't believe in bad luck, he wasn't afflicted with such stupidity. Only the superstitious got back luck. He didn't believe in good luck either.

He reached into his jacket pocket and removed the rolled up sheet of paper, laying it on the table. He'd finish his coffee and pie and ask Simone if she'd tape it to the front window.

She would. She seemed kind.

He looked at the face that haunted him and smiled, shoring back the grief that always wanted to pour forth over the Formica and faux leather.

Tather looked away from the dour faced news anchor and concentrated on the pie before him. He picked up the spoon and carved off a corner of crust. He lifted it and shovelled it into his mouth. It may have been the last slice of a two day old pie but it was still delicious. Maybe the aging had done it good, maturing and marinating the flavours. It was worth the wait. With his tongue he squashed the morsel onto the roof of his mouth, pressing and savouring the tang of blackberries. He took a sip of hot coffee then looked out of the window, his taste buds delighting with the sensations. A golden brown moth fluttered and bumped its way into the window trying to get at the faux moons inside. Tather looked beyond the navigationally confused insect and tried to find the motor home resting under the darkened shade of the dying oak tree. He couldn't see it from this angle. The fencing at the back of the diner that housed the delivery entrance, the recycling and any waste hid it from view.

Susannah would have liked this; chatting over a hot drink with a sugary lump of goodness to share before them. This was how he'd imagined the autumn quarter of his life. Even if they'd spent the day together, they'd still enjoy the moment and find something to chat about. An old joke, a favourite anecdote or maybe just people watch and giggle at their idiosyncrasies and foibles.

But after a while conversation would have become forced and awkward, they'd glare at the silences in each other's eyes and wonder …

. . . you're either thinking exactly the same as me or something I don't even want to consider . . . The golden times weren't to be. Life always gets in the way of plans and intentions.

When something like that happens you can't fix it. It's impossible. It's a sinking vessel with a deck below the water line but you keep bailing and pumping out because you believe it's a ship worth saving. You can spit on a wound all you like to stop a haemorrhage, but pretty soon you're blinded by all the blood and you feel yourself slipping away to nothing despite all your wasted efforts.

He wondered why he was here. What is the point exactly?

Am I a joke? Or a lesson to others, perhaps?

Where do I fit in exactly?

Because it beats the alternative and you hold on to hope, he kept telling himself. Because apart from memories and photos, that's all you've got left; scraps of fading paper and painful nostalgia that hurts too much to even consider.

You hold on to hope for as long as you can. You never stop giving up.

Well . . . some do.

What if an electrical fault sparks a house fire and you lose everything but the clothes on your back? Luckily; if you could call it luck you were out for an anniversary dinner and you survive unscathed. But you lose all of your favourite books, all the stupid little gifts you've bought each other and all the photos you've ever taken. Every picture you'd ever taken, gone, flashed up and away in a blue-green chemical instant, to nothing more than white ashes and a wisp of smoke.

It happens.

He had his wallet on him. He had one photo in it that was truly his. He had the fear that what if his memory started to go along with his knees the way age affects us all, then what? They'd have pretty much nothing but the dust of memories filling their minds. He'd be left holding a photo of a stranger.

Friends had rallied round and brought photos of them together, often just background artists in other folk's memories. It's wasn't the same. They weren't their photographs. It felt like cheating; a pirated movie of their lives.

Tather kept himself sharp. He read, did Sudoku at breakfast much to Susannah's annoyance. But it kept his mind limber. He had to concentrate on something. Anything but . . .

He even took up sketching in secret, drawing from memory alone, but it felt like he was squeezing the iron from his blood. It was hard; the pictures were pitiful manifestations and never did his imagination justice. He never showed Susannah, he hid them away in the attic beneath the insulation. Sure he was disappointed, but he wasn't going to chide himself for the efforts he made. Sure, the pictures held some resemblance, but he wasn't going to embarrass himself and upset Susannah on her birthday.

Nancy Sinatra interrupted Elvis's warbling and started off with a strutting attitude into 'These Boots Are Made for Walking'. Then the door to the diner opened, and a gust blew in that chilled Elliott Tather so much he was almost convinced it was winter outside and not a sweaty late August night. Tather didn't know it yet but the world as he'd come to know and let grind against him would never be the same again.

***

They couldn't see Tather where he was sat, for his booth was tucked in around the corner where the kitchen block ended. A wooden cupboard filled with spare plates and cutlery, topped with a bank of condiments hid him further from view. Tather glanced round and looked through the glass of a near empty jug of red and blue striped straws, watching them walk in through a scratched lens of glass.

The man was tall; close to seven foot, ducking his black ponytailed head slightly as he stepped through the door. He wore a pair of Aviator shades even though it was near full dark outside. Tather looked outside. The young family's Range Rover had pulled out of the car park. All that remained was his motor home and what he assumed to be the waitress's Volvo. Where had the tall stranger parked? He never saw any vehicles pull in. Maybe he'd been daydreaming through their arrival.

The intriguing stranger wore a thin, dark leather coat; even under the glare of the fluorescents Tather couldn't tell if it was grey, black or dark brown. The strange coloured coat carried down to the tall man's ankles where they met a pair of dusty rigger boots that looked like they'd seen a thousand battles in the last hundred years. His face was all angles, as if severe chunks had been shaved off during his gestation in the womb to produce such sharp and definite features. His mouth looked packed, making him look like he'd just come from dental surgery and still had a mouthful of cotton balls.

The tall, gaunt man made his way to the counter as the door opened behind him. A young woman strode in with an eager confidence; she had a bounce in her step which unnerved Tather. She looked high on something, maybe too much Red Bull or pep pills. She wore a burgundy lace dress with a plunging neck line that showed off too much of her young firm breasts, far too dressy for this establishment. Maybe they were in costume or on the way home from a concert Tather surmised, embarrassed by the vague awakening in his underwear. It was natural, she was beautiful, but something about her scared him a little. She was already smiling.

He kept his eye on them as the door opened a third time. The tall man tapped the bell on the counter with flick of his wrist, then leant over the till and looked down the galley, intruding his presence.

'Service,' he called out in a theatrical chime.

The main door closed and Tather had to doubly concentrate on what he saw. He blinked. He blinked again to assess the deception. He tapped his tongue on the roof of his mouth as if testing the thought that some hallucinogenic compound or bitter poison had tainted the apple and blackberry pie. He tasted nothing but sugared fruit and sweet pie crust.

He tongue must be lying to him.

What he saw was real, his world fell apart as his mind carried back through the months, the years, the tears, the fights, the insomnia, the searching, the storm drains and the posters.

His heart crystallised, frozen between beats. In panic he raised his hand to thump his chest in an effort to awaken the paralysed muscle. It hung still in front of him, fused in midair. He couldn't move. He drew breath and felt his pulse quicken, telling him he was alive and this was real.

The counter bell was still ringing in his ears as his hypnotised mind was cast back to . . .

Ketchup on Everything

Ketchup on Everything

. . . his gaze became fixed upon the tiny ripples in the little pool. It was empty. He called out his name, waited a beat for a response, and then headed deeper into the garden. He searched the shed, the bush at the back of the garden and the gap down the side of the garage which he'd blocked off with an old fence panel to keep him from exploring the dangerous stacks of bricks and roof tiles that were stored there, left over from the previous owners.

Nothing.

A thorn pierced his heart with an abrupt coldness, pricking the comfortable life he'd forged for his family. Elliott enjoyed his nine-to-five existence and the humour he held with his colleagues. His home life was perfect with a doting family and a sex life that seemed to improve with each anniversary. They had two cars, a pension pot and plans to buy a holiday home abroad. Susannah and he rarely argued, and both regularly swam to complement their clean bill of health. Life was good. He had no complaints, but he'd give up all of that to know that his one true joy wasn't missing from the back garden.

From the kitchen, the sound of the radio playing the new song by 'Nirvana' beat through the open door and into the garden. Elliott tried to tune it out and listen over the thundering drone that filled his ears.

Ketchup on Everything

Drawing his hands in a cup around his mouth to help amplify his call, he bellowed again, tiring from the impromptu game of hide and seek.

He shouted his name,

Nothing.

A brief pang of panic ballooned within, betraying the wholesome June sunshine that enlightened their little garden. The pang expanded, pouring ice water over his Friday afternoon hijinks with his son.

He was playing a game; please let him be playing a game.

Elliott Tather headed back to check the house.

He stopped on the patio, the creeping chill snaking an icicle down his spine. It spoke a horrible language of truth and possibility that made his guts gurgle and squirm. His mind reeled; rapidly computing what he should do next, which direction he chose could mean everything or nothing.

He'd had a great day planned, a little splash in the pool in the morning. Maybe even make a cardboard fort in the afternoon. Spaghetti Bolognaise for tea. His favourite.

Susannah would return from work and after they'd eaten, they'd all pile on the sofa under a big blanket and watch a video. He adored the cosy moments with his family.

It wasn't to be.

The back gate which should have been bolted at the top was wide open; Evan Tather was gone.

Elliott rushed towards the gate, eying it with mild disgust at its failure to secure his household. The top bolt was undone. Evan could have never reached it. He'd always meant to padlock it, but with the amount of times they used the side gate they'd spend half of the time locking and unlocking it.

A *ball ache*, he'd called it, regretting his laziness now.

Elliott Tather had realised soon after becoming a father that his outlook on life had changed. The revs slipped up a gear as he sped towards his own mortality. With a child, he realised that life and his mark upon the world would continue on without him. The time he had left had become precious, and he was fully aware of the saying that youth is wasted on the young, paraphrasing it in his mind as youths don't know the time they're wasting. He relished every moment with his son and harboured a great disinterest in doing chores and general maintenance of his home, hence the lack of discipline with securing a simple padlock.

A malignant regret howled within and he increased his speed down the passageway that ran between his house and his neighbours' then broke into a run towards the road.

He called his son's name.

West then East, he bellowed down the street with his hands cupped around his mouth to act as a megaphone. The afternoon was empty of human interference. People were at work, not at home. Apart from one or two housewives, he was alone.

Tather shouted, roared and pleaded with his son to stop playing this awful game. He headed back into the house to call Susannah, stubbing his toe on the front step as he rushed. If he'd waited a few seconds longer he would have seen and not just heard the Volkswagen van with blacked out windows pull out and drive towards the junction and turn left out of his life.

***

Susannah told him she was heading home and in the meantime told him to call the police. Without saying goodbye to his wife, he frantically did as he was told, pressing down the receiver on the cordless with a fumbled clatter before dialling the police. His voice a nervous machine gun of words, barrelling out syllables as he tried to give the police as much information as possible in the least amount of time.

He headed back into the garden, scouring for any sign of Evan. He stopped at the side passage of the house, haunted by what he saw. Still wet from the pool, Evan's drying footprints walked away from him, through the gate and towards the front of the house. He hadn't noticed them on the first pass, so shivered as he followed their trail. Leading off in the direction of the road, they'd already started to fade as they were in the process of evaporating on the sun-baked driveway. The track ended here. Elliott sunk to his knees on the hard concrete. This was where the police found him, crying tears that fell and evaporated away on the hot concrete just as his son's footsteps had done so moments before.

***

With a squeal of tyres, Susannah arrived back home not long after the police. The couple embraced then called friends and relatives to rally around bodies. A few came round, while others took to their cars and patrolled the streets. Police tape was wound out across the driveway to block out visitors and prints were swiftly taken from the garden gate. They both gave their fingerprints to rule them out from any alien markings that happened to be found on the premise.

He and Susannah sat on the sofa, distraught but still expecting Evan to walk through the door oblivious to the commotion he'd caused. They gripped each other's inked fingers almost hatefully while the police asked questions about Evan. Both Elliott and Susannah cried freely and without abandon. To soak up their grief, a box of tissues was soon emptied with each wracking sniffle.

'What was he wearing?' the white haired officer asked. The Tathers got the impression he'd being drafted in to show that someone with experience was on the case. He'd introduced himself as Sergeant Henry Hollins, a bristly white moustache that commanded authority hung from his top lip like a devoted albino caterpillar. Reassuringly, he looked the part.

'Blue swimming shorts and a *Ninja Turtles* t-shirt.'

'He was in the back garden.'

'Yes, in the little swimming pool. We bought it last weekend.'

'And the gate was locked?'

'Yes, he couldn't have reached the top bolt without a step.'

'Did you hear anything?'

'No. I was inside making lunch.

'Are you sure?'

'I told you; no.'

'What is it you do Mr Tather?' Hollins asked.

'I work as an underwriter at Henderson Insurance and my wife is a receptionist for a haulage company. We've been alternating days off to care for Evan.'

'Did you argue this morning?'

'My wife and I?'

'No. You and your son.'

'No. Not at all. We were quite happy until all of this.' Elliott stopped. He longed for a sip of water, but daren't ask for one for it would deny the situation time that it needed more that he required dampness in his throat. He swallowed dry and continued, finding his order of words

'Evan hasn't been all that well since Tuesday that's why he's not being at school. He'd lost his appetite and he's had trouble sleeping with the headaches he's had. He was at the doctors yesterday to get his bloods done, to see if they can explain his lethargy. We're still waiting on the results.' Elliott bit his lip. His son's mysterious illness had shifted down his list of worries.

'Do you think his disappearance might be down to his illness? Sometimes if people are ill they choose to be alone.'

'I don't think so. Today he said he felt a little better and wouldn't mind playing outside, that's why he was in the pool. He wanted some sun, so I went in to make some dinner. I went to use the toilet then I came back into the kitchen, plated up our lunch then went outside to fetch Evan.'

'Any strangers in the area, anybody you don't recognize?'

'I don't remember.'

'Are the police looking?' Susannah asked, steering the conversation around to finding facts of the future, rather than the past.

'We're making enquires,' said Hollins

'Like what?' she pushed.

'We're calling round on possible suspects that live in the area, the picture of Evan you gave us will be shown on tonight's news and hopefully the major newspapers in tomorrow's paper if they pull their fingers out. We'll get officers out with copies to show to the public at shopping centres. It's important that we get Evan's face into the minds of the public as early as possible.'

'What about roadblocks?' Elliott asked.

'We haven't the man power I'm afraid.'

'You're afraid?' Susannah cut in. 'Our son is missing.'

'I'm sorry, what I meant was I can't draft any more officers in from neighbouring counties until tomorrow, but in the meantime we're concentrating on door to door enquires of possible suspects. I'm stretched as it is at the moment.' Hollins spread his palms to illustrate his point.

'Worst case scenario. If he has been kidnapped, and there is something wrong with him do you really think they'll care about Evan's condition or will they just let him die?' Elliott said frankly.

'That's a matter we'll have to deal with later,' Hollins replied.

'No it's not, because if we don't find him we won't have to deal with it, will we?'

This silenced all breath in the room.

Hollins was stumped. A bad situation was getting worse and worse and despite his years on the force, he admitted that he'd never dealt with a kidnapping before. Missing children yes, but they'd all turned up safe and well after an argument with their parents or problems at school. He'd never had a pure vanishing before.

Hollins asked for a list of friends and relatives and their addresses, then left, leaving behind an officer posted on the front door. The search would continue in the morning with more men, including volunteers working a wider area. Their relatives left, their friends left, all dumbfounded and at a loss of what to say. Some offered to search the street in their cars. Both Elliott and Susannah thanked them kindly.

Once everyone had left, Elliott stood up and walked into the kitchen and poured himself a straight whisky. He knocked it back with a stinging gulp, and then took another, more eager swig straight from the bottle. It didn't help his dry throat at all, but it spilt fire on the abject numbness he felt throughout his person. He placed the glass by the sink and spotted the plate. The cheddar on toast he'd made for Evan's lunch remained cold and uneaten on the worktop. The cheese topping now a yellow puddle of thick grease, the splodge of ketchup had turned into a dark red skin that had shrivelled as the day wore on.

A knock at the front door filled him with a sudden, strange hope that both excited and terrified him. He looked at his wife for a fraction of a second with a wild eyed anticipation then ran and tore the door open, expecting both a police officer with grave news and Evan himself looking sheepish.

It was Joshua Greenway and Lilly Vaughn, two of Evan's friends from school, still dressed in uniform. They jumped back from the violence of which the front door was thrown open, both gasping with fright.

'Sorry kids, I didn't mean to make you jump,' Elliott apologised.

'Huh huh, no worries Mister Tather,' Joshua said as he recovered. He looked back to the policeman at the end of the drive. 'How's Evan feeling? Is everything okay?'

'Okay,' Elliott said, wondering why the syllables had even left his mouth. At the end of the drive the policeman turned around and viewed the scene with something more than dismay, beyond pity. *How could this be easy for anyone? Telling your son's best friends that he'd vanished from the face of the earth. That was what Elliott read on the officer's face.*

Susannah joined him at the front door to greet the guests, and burst into a torrent of tears.

The children took a step back at the sight of an adult breaking down before them, fearing she might pop. Elliott's own lips quivered and he struggled to dam the grief that wanted to spout forth.

He grimaced and sucked at his lips to steel his jaw. Susannah fell into him, he held her up as she buried her head in his chest.

'Evan has disappeared. We don't know where he's gone.'

'Oh no,' the two young children cried out in unison. Lilly held her hands to her mouth.

'Shall we tell our parents?' Joshua asked.

'If you wouldn't mind Josh, the more people know the better, the police are out looking for him now.'

'Do you need volunteers?' Lilly asked.

'We don't know what to do yet, it's only been a few hours. The police said stay here in case he comes back.'

'We'll tell our parents. I hope he turns up soon.' Joshua looked at a folder he'd been holding and held it out to Elliott Tather.

'What's this?'

'It's ET's homework.' Evan's friends had christened him ET because of his initials. 'Mrs Goddard asked us to drop it off.'

Elliott took the folder and stashed it under his arm.

'Thanks guys, much appreciated.

'I can't believe it. Where could he be?' Lilly shook her head, she looked sick.

'We'll find him Mrs Tather. Me and Lilly will help. We'll get the school involved. Mr Horner will do something.'

Elliott nodded, he couldn't find the words as the tears started to burn his eyes, the grief creating a salty clog at the back of his throat. He closed the door without further utterance.

Leading his distraught wife back to the kitchen, Elliott dropped the folder on the kitchen table and embraced his wife trying to crush the grief from her.

'What are we going to do? He's gone!' Susannah cried.

'He'll be back. Just wait. He's wandered off, that's all.' Elliott patted her back to reassure her.

'But what if he doesn't?'

'Try not to think like that.'

'I can't, it's real!'

'Don't . . .'

'He's not coming back! Some crazy pervert has taken our son Elliott. He's gone!'

Elliott let go of his wife, then with a roar of movement, he started ripping cupboards open, raking out the contents onto the kitchen floor, broken glass, flour and sauces littered the floor within the minute of tortured lunacy. He bounded upstairs with a fretful howl, whilst Susannah remained slumped on the sofa in a grief induced stupor. Every towel was whipped out of the airing cupboard; he upturned the beds, emptied toy boxes and de-cluttered the wardrobes.

The police sentry remained outside. He wasn't to interfere in emotional turmoil. He was merely there for presence. He peered through the window. Once he saw that the violence wasn't aimed at Mrs Tather he resumed his duty. Elliott Tather carried on his tearing apart of his own home in an anguished and bitter discord.

He even pulled himself into the loft space and blindly screamed Evan's name into every corner, finding nothing but startled spiders that retreated into cracks in the mortar and beneath the irritating woolly blanket of yellow insulation.

Tather would have knocked the house down brick by brick if his wife hadn't stopped him with a vice embrace when he fell out of the loft wild eyed and frantic. He wanted to tear the world apart in his search, not just for Evan, but for forgiveness as well. He was here when Evan went missing, it had been his watch. He couldn't forgive himself for that, only the sight of his son before him would do that.

'I can't just sit and do nothing,' he wept.
'I know.'
'We have to do something.'
'I know.'

'I mean, we're his parents. What do we do?'

'We need to rest. We should try and get some sleep. We haven't got many options right now.'

They fell into each other, weeping and screaming their only comforts. It wasn't that it felt good to let go, it was the release of doing something, anything. Somehow, his tortured animal cries were cathartic; the burst of energy from his lungs venting a dangerous, self-loathing pressure that threatened to boil his mind dry of reason, hope and love.

***

Elliott Tather didn't sleep. Or couldn't. It didn't matter. At 3 AM he started to clear up the chaos he'd caused in the kitchen, dumping the haunted cheese on toast and the rest of the mess into black bags whilst Susannah slept a pitiful toss of sleep beside the phone.

He tidied upstairs, dutifully folding towels and hanging up his wife's clothes back in their rightful place. He placed all Evan's toys back in the toy boxes and the books carefully back in order on the shelves. Anything broken he binned. Evidently, Evan wasn't playing a cruel trick by hiding in some dark corner. He wished it to be true and he'd keep on wishing.

In the main bedroom, he released a picture of Evan taken on his last birthday from its frame. He found a sheet of paper and a thick black marker pen, got dressed then took a walk to the 24 hour petrol station down the road. Elliott managed a grunt towards the young policeman on his doorstep as he left, managing to utter the syllable, 'Walk', before heading off alone into the chill morning fog, the swathes of grey eating him, then his shadow.

Half an hour later he was back home with three hundred copies of the same text and image repeated across the stack of sheets.

> Missing since Friday.
> Evan Tather
> Age 8
> If you know where he is or you have seen him, please contact Abcastle police
> or his parents Elliott and Susannah Tather,
> who miss him with all their hearts.

Elliott had included his home phone number at the bottom, beneath the now black and white birthday picture of Evan. In it he was grinning, seconds away from blowing out the eight burning candles on his pirate ship birthday cake. The photocopy had lost colour and a little of its quality. But the cheek and charm of his son remained, still smiling at him from six months ago. Elliott stared at his son, willing for the front door to open and him to walk back into his life. He stared into his eyes, trying to somehow connect with him psychically and determine his location.

Elliott Tather kicked himself for not putting on Evan's eye colour.

Christ what colour are his eyes?

Blue. His eyes were blue. Just like his old man.

He spent the next hour and a half writing on with a deteriorating scrawl in the top corner

His eyes are blue

Well before number two hundred and ninety-nine, it had become a maddening task that was essential to his sanity and well-being. Each correction was like plucking a splinter from his mind. His hand was cramped up by the time he reached the end, knuckles fused claw-like around the pen. He had to physically pull his fingers apart with his other hand to bend his hooked fingers back straight.

The irritating notion of describing his hair colour occurred to him as an annoying afterthought, but he dismissed it. You could tell from the photo that Evan's hair was dark. Besides, if Evan had been taken, hair clippers, dye and wigs could be utilised in order to disguise his son's appearance he thought grimly. Eyes were a different matter. Taking Evan to the dentist was enough of a challenge, let alone trying to slip in contact lenses. They could always slip a pair of sunglasses on him should they take him out in public. He shuddered at the thought of *they*.

They were real.

His agents of misery.

Stealers of his sunshine.

Ketchup on Everything

That's it, keep thinking he's still alive. Keep hoping. Don't think the worst, even though it hung around the corners of his mind, an interfering stranger offering dark glimpses of what could be. Elliott didn't need that.

Evan was three when Elliott realised that no decent parent ever comes to terms with the fact that one day, their beautiful bundle of careless joy will perish. They say it's a tragedy if a child dies before their parents. It isn't a tragedy. It was far worse. Widows lose husbands and orphans lose parents, but life goes on. Tragedy doesn't even come close to describe the loss of a child. It pained him to think of a word to sum it up. He couldn't. There wasn't one. Hell is just a made up place anyway.

Evan was alive. Evan was missing. It was only a matter of time before they found him.

Time would pass. They would find him.

He considered the possibility of a ransom note. If one was mailed anonymously to them demanding cash, what would they sell?

Everything and anything to get Evan back in their arms.

Kidneys, eyes, testicles.

Everything. He'd sell his soul to get Evan back.

Elliott Tather found a backpack and placed the three hundred posters inside. He searched the garage, finding a stapler he'd used last year to re-felt the shed roof. He found the big box of 1000 one-inch staples and placed these in the back pack as well.

Feeling a clawing dryness in his throat, Elliott Tather popped the kettle on and made a strong coffee. He needed to wet his throat with something and whisky wasn't the way forward.

As he was taking his first sip, Susannah creaked in from the living room like Death personified. The whites of her eyes were red raw with despair. The tops of her cheeks were smeared with a sorrowful charcoal smudge, further proving her exhaustion. Elliott became caught in her gaze and stared deeply at his wife and into her pupils that seemed to have become empty and beyond black; a nothing, a hollow, a space devoid of all light and joy and soul. Now spent of energy, they seemed incapable of reflecting even the brightest glow.

She approached him and cried empty tears, gripping him with fervent anguish, her blunt, chewed fingernails digging into his back as if she were clinging onto a crumbling, vertical ledge. He was the cusp stopping her from tipping into complete and utter insanity. She needed him more than ever, despite the fact he felt powerless and impotent at how their life had spiralled away from them in less than twenty four hours. They needed to become firm and not let themselves drown in melancholy.

'I'll make you a coffee,' he said when she loosened her grip a little; 'it'll do you good.' She nodded soundlessly.

They stood in the kitchen, sipping from steaming mugs and silently contemplating each other from the corner of their eyes, both unwilling to talk but both frothing with questions.

After she finished her coffee, Susannah spoke first.

'Couldn't you sleep either?'

'I had to do something. I got cleaned up and then I made these.'

Elliott reached into the backpack and pulled out a poster and handed it to his wife.

Susannah held the sheet of paper in front of her, consuming the information her husband had scrawled across the page. She peeked into the bag and saw the stack of A4. Thumbing through, she quickly realised that the same text and image was copied on every single one.

'Won't the police be doing this?'

'I know they are, but I have to do something. The inaction is killing me.'

'This is a good idea.' Susannah smiled, her black eyes brightening.

'We have to do something. I can't wait for the police to not do enough. What if somebody the police miss sees one of our posters? We wouldn't know unless we try.'

'What you planning on doing with them?'

'Stick them on every street corner, every lamp post, telegraph pole and shop window I can find, then come back print some more.'

She didn't smile, but her face glowed a little with what could be called hope.

'Got another stapler?'

***

They told the sentry of their plan, not giving him a choice as he insisted they stay and wait for Sergeant Hollins to return. Time was an issue, and they didn't have time for protocol. They'd leave the front door open in case he wanted to use the toilet or make a drink. The young officer shifted uncomfortably upon the front step, seemingly eager to take them up on their offer, giving them kind thanks and a nod.

They split the posters. Elliott gave his wife the stapler, whilst he took a hammer and box of tacks. They each took with them a roll of Sellotape and headed out onto the streets, venturing east and west to cover different sides of town. Elliott covered the high street and the western industrial park, whilst Susannah did suburbia, the housing developments and the council blocks. They didn't have time to knock on every single door in town. This was their best option.

If he could nail to it, he did. If he could tape to it, he would. Every second shop he came across he asked the owners who happily posted the missing poster in windows. One corner shop owner stipulated that there was a two-fifty a week charge for adverts in the window. Once Elliott had shown and explained the photo, the shop keeper relented and agreed to keep the poster with apologetic waves of his hands.

With his backpack empty of posters and only a handful of tacks left, Elliott returned home to find Sergeant Henry Hollins waiting for him on his doorstep. The sentry had been apparently relieved of his duty. Elliott didn't ask of his whereabouts.

'Morning Mister Tather,' Hollins greeted him.

'Hey,' was all he could manage. His voice was hoarse and brittle, his lips chapped from dehydration and fatigue.

'The search teams have been out since dawn.'

'Good. Anything?'

'Nothing yet. Early days.'

'Is that all you came here for?'

'I wanted to keep you informed of events, regardless of the detail.'

'Thank you. Sorry if I'm a bit curt with you, but I've not slept. I've been posting missing posters since about seven o'clock.'

'We'll be doing that as well. We've been going door to door.'

'I know, but I want permanent pictures on every street corner. I can't sit and do nothing.'

'I understand. The local news ran a plea at six this morning, television and radio. There's a good chance the national news might run a piece this afternoon. Fingers crossed, I can't make guarantees just yet, but the BBC might send a reporter round for a few words. The first twenty-four hours are about as much exposure as possible. We need to get Evan into people's minds whilst it's still fresh.'

'Thank you. Would you like a coffee?' Elliott asked as a police car pulled up outside. Hollins stepped off the porch and down the driveway. A

WPC stepped out of the passenger side and stood next Hollins.

'Afraid not. My expertise is needed on door-to-door. We need every available man if we want to find your son. I'll try to organise a press conference for tomorrow if that's okay? In the mean time get some sleep. It's the best you can do for yourselves. You don't want to burn out.'

Hollins got inside the car, and the driver took him away into the brightening blue morning.

***

Elliott offered the policewoman the chance of a hot drink, which she gratefully accepted. He was handing her the steaming mug when Susannah returned. Her face was taut with concern and barren of smiles. Elliott ushered her inside. Wordless and vanquished of energy, they embraced and fell upon the sofa. Sleep fell upon them as if a cloud of anaesthetic waited in the room.

They slept a deep and dreamless black, a nothing that saved their unconscious sanities from any memory plagued by thoughts of Evan.

They were awoken in the afternoon from an incessant knock at the front door. It was Hollins. They'd found a body.

***

Elliott thought about his parents. Both dead early from a bad lifestyle before Evan was born. Susannah was in the same boat having lost both of hers within months of each other last year. In their case it was failed hearts broken by loss. With no one else to turn to, he felt like they were facing this alone .

'It's not Evan. The body is seriously decomposed, maybe even two years or so. We found her in some undergrowth by the motorway.' Hollins stared at the coffee cup he cradled in his thin fingers. He seemed to be savouring the steam that rose towards his face.

'A she?' Susannah asked. She held her husband's hand with a fraught determination, her grip hard and cold in his.

'The deceased is taller than Evan, and a wedding ring with a diamond would indicate that it is indeed a female. Plus the clothes, despite their condition appeared to belong to a female. But then we're never sure until the lab boys have done their tests.'

'Why are you telling us this? If it's not Evan, what news is this to us?'

'We have to tell the media something, and I'd rather you hear from me than from the newspapers. I want you to know that we're doing everything we can think of to help you.'

'I know you are Mister Hollins.'

'Please, call me Henry.'

'Thank you Henry.' Susannah squeezed out a smile that aged her around the eyes.

'Apart from that how's the search going?' Elliott asked.

'I've currently got officers searching the homes of your friends and relatives. It's our routine, so we have to extinguish every avenue. At this moment nobody is a suspect, unless you can think of anyone in particular. Anybody with a past? Anybody you've had a bad feeling about in the slightest? Anything at all?'

'We're nice people Mister Holl . . . I mean Henry. I think Susannah's brother John Jacobs had a drink driving ban a few years back. Apart from that we socialise with good, hardworking people. We don't know all of our neighbours' secrets, nor their deviancies. I can honestly say I really don't think anybody we know has taken Evan.' Elliott sighed then leant back into the sofa before admitting. 'We don't have enemies. I think this is just a random stranger.'

'A stranger who knew Evan would be in your back garden?'

'Maybe he heard him playing?'

'He?'

'I'm guessing here. That's all police work is until you find something concrete.'

'That's right I'm afraid.' Hollins took a sip of his drink and then placed it upon a coaster on the coffee table. He spent a moment watching the ripples settle.

'I guess they're the lucky ones,' Susannah said.

'Who?' Hollins asked.

'That girl's family. At least they'll know what happened to her. Strangely I'm happy for them.'

Ketchup on Everything

'Grief is a strange thing,' Hollins said sagely. He seemed to be well versed in dealing with bad news. Elliott had to hand it to Hollins; he'd been a champion so far.

'Right, I'm going. I'm pulling a double shift today. If you'd like me to organise a counsellor, contact the station and we can arrange something. I'd recommend it. It does help to talk to someone.'

Hollins stood. Elliott and Susannah did the same. He motioned to leave. Susannah stopped him and kissed Hollins on the cheek. He smiled and regarded Elliott kindly in the eye.

'Thank you,' she whispered.

Hollins smiled again, nodded to them both, then left.

The only good news Hollins brought came a week later and was of the young woman they'd found instead of Evan. She was called Fiona McKlespie. Her husband George had stabbed her lover to death with a bread knife and strangled her after discovering they were having an affair. . Whilst Fiona was cast amongst the detritus of the nearby motorway, the lover's body was found in similar circumstances in the next county. George McKlespie had pulled up on the hard shoulder in the middle of the night, dragged his wife's corpse from the boot of their car and dumped her over the railing. She flipped, flopped, rolled and tumbled to the bottom of the embankment where she laid as sustenance for wildlife until the disappearance of Evan Tather.

George had reported his wife missing, as any good husband should, feigning that she'd run away with her lover and taken a suitcase with her.

Upon being told of his wife's demise, George McKlespie broke down and confessed everything, even the fact that he later dumped a suitcase of his wife's clothes in a river that lead out to sea. He would eventually receive two life sentences for all his efforts. Not a month into his sentence he picked a fight with a group of prisoners, resulting in his demise. The autopsy revealed that massive amounts of haemorrhaging had occurred leading to fatal blood loss. In reality George McKlespie had been stamped to death after picking a fight with four inmates much bigger than him.

Having followed the murder trial that had briefly touched his life, Elliott was strangely pleased that at least some good had come from his son's disappearance. He seldom smiled after he lost Evan. Then one day Dr Meadows came round with what was the final nail in the metaphoric coffin that contained the memory of his son. After that day, he didn't feel like smiling ever again.

***

A priest came and gave them wise words that meant nothing in the grand scheme of things.

'Your grief is your grief. No one can take that away from you.'

Ketchup on Everything

Why not? They can cure headaches, prolong erections and take dispossessed youths to acid tinged dimensions. Why can't they invent a drug to turn off grief without sending you catatonic?

Alcohol numbed it, dulled reasoning and then flared the anger to a furnace like annoyance in the resulting hangover. An induced coma might help.

Religion gave no reasons or answers.

Evan's school had held an assembly that he attended alone. Susannah had every intention of attending, but her streaked mascara and wracking sobs gave Elliott reason to excuse her.

'You stay here. Have some time to yourself. We need to be strong in front of the children and I don't think you've got that strength today.'

She nodded in agreement and wiped off the black wash of makeup with a kitchen towel. Elliott hugged her and headed out of the door unaccompanied. A dark spidery smudge bled onto the shoulder of his best suit.

In the reception area he shook everyone's hand in a blur of passing faces; his thanks became a solemn, automatic response as everyone offered their grey faced condolences. Children filtered into hall; some whispered, whilst others hadn't a clue as to who he was.

Once everyone was seated, Mr Horner, the head teacher had implored any pupil to come forward with any information, no matter how small. Elliott hoped, but didn't expect any of the children to step forward. He wasn't disappointed. The children remained stoic, silent and glum in the sunlit hall, as to be excepted when one of their well loved schoolmates vanishes without a trace.

After Mr Horner dismissed the hall, blonde angel Lilly Vaughn broke from the ranks of children filing through the back doors, her locks bouncing through the sunrays, and rushed over to Elliott, where he stood with the morose line of staff that hummed with coffee breath and cigarette smoke.

He expected her to say something and opened his mouth to say hello, instead Lilly nearly knocked him over and threw her arms around his waist. Unsure of what to do he rested his hands on her shoulders and lightly patted her back. Those remaining in the hall turned their gazes to them.

'I saw him Mister Tather. He came to me last night. In my dreams. He's still alive, but he can't get to you. He wants to. He's trying. But he can't.'

Lilly squeezed again. Elliott squeezed back and clenched his jaw to stop his emotions exploding in front of the kids. These were Evan's friends, look how strong they were being. He should try to do the same.

'I don't know where he is, but he's alive.'
'Thanks Lilly.'
'I want him to come back. I want to marry Evan when I grow up.'
'Really? He never told me.'
'I haven't told him yet.'
'One day you will.'

'I know.'

A few teachers smiled. Mrs Loveday, Evan's teacher smiled and cried at the same time.

Lilly let go.

'I just wanted you to know that. He's okay.'

She fell back into the crowd and became lost in the faces. Elliott knew it was a child's overactive imagination seeking wish fulfilment, but he himself wished it was true.

Lilly Vaughn had a dream about his son, living and in the future. Elliott needed to do everything in his power to make it come true.

***

It had been four weeks since the disappearance of Evan Tather. The night before, the BBC's Crimewatch programme had run a re-enactment of Evan Tather and his last moments with his father. The boy they used was similar to his son in stature and hair colour, but failed to capture his son's handsomeness. Watching the young boy act reminded Elliott of his son's own acting efforts in the school nativity play. Playing one of the wise men, a five year old Evan's turn came to recite his line of *"and I have brought frankincense,"* instead he uttered, *"Daddy, I need a poo."*

The crowd erupted into donkey braying guffaws, whilst Evan remained utterly bewildered to the amusement he'd caused.

In response to the Crimewatch show, several apparent witnesses came forward, but nothing looked positive that early on. One incendiary journalist from one of the red tops had insisted that the police make Elliott Tather take a polygraph test. A few like-minded lunatics listened, but nothing came of it.

The search teams had been called off the day before and that was the last time he would ever speak to Henry Hollins, with the sergeant explaining that it wasn't an economical use of manpower, according to his superiors. Everybody had to answer to somebody. As he shuffled down the driveway to the patrol car, Elliott was sure the elderly sergeant was crying.

Susannah gave up with her efforts soon after. The morning Dr Meadows made his appearance she was out at work with the defence that the nine to five helped take her mind off her everything.

He didn't believe her.

Regardless of the world churning outside his own, Elliott had been out all morning examining storm drains with a torch, a stick and a set of waders he'd purchased from a tackle shop that very week for that very purpose. Though, he was no closer to buying a suit for Lilly's wedding.

The incessant rain had held him off before noon, he'd searched four storm drains, but several more dotted alongside a country track still had his attention to gain. He'd found nothing more exciting than plastic bags, tree branches and a dead ginger tomcat, which he laid to rest in a shallow grave; because that's what you do with dead things. We give them peace from the sky and the rest of the world.

If the rain held off in the afternoon he'd return before the daylight faded.

Work had kindly given him leave, so Elliott Tather had spent the time wisely, not wasting a moment of daylight. Every day since they'd found the body of Fiona McKlespie, Elliott had been out with the search teams. Although at times he was often on his own, the end of the official search had done nothing to faze him. He carried on from sun up to sun down. He had a few devoted friends and family members who helped out when they could, but their efforts soon faded. He didn't blame them for not answering the phone. They had their own lives to worry about. And besides, it wasn't them who'd lost a child. They owed him nothing, though he was grateful for the help and time they'd given. He'd secretly hoped that Henry Hollins would have joined him. But he continued alone.

'I'll be fine,' he used to tell Susannah when she fretted.

Every night he dreamt about finding Evan. Sometimes he was okay. Elliott would turn a dream projected corner and Evan would be stood there. He'd mouth *"Hey Daddy"* soundlessly and run towards his father with a wide, bright smile. He never made it. Elliott always woke up seconds before his son reached his open arms. Other times, would be the bad dreams. Dark drains, flooded corridors, derelict basements with creeping damp and anywhere else you'd expect to find a body formed the dreamscape. The body would always have its back to him, sometimes floating. Elliott would reach out and turn it over, knowing it would be his son. The bloated sack of flesh would flop over, Evan's pale and mottled cheeks bubbling with dancing maggots as he smiled and bellowed loud and clear "*Hey Daddy*."

Strangely, Elliott never awoke from these dreams. He was made to suffer them until he awoke baking with a slick sheen of hot sweat bleeding into the crumpled sheets.

Did Lilly Vaughn dream such horrors? Elliott hoped not.

Once he awoke with hot, bitter vomit in his mouth. He swallowed it, disgusted and sorry for himself. He'd been dreaming of the faceless bogey man who'd taken his son, a character who never showed himself, but was always there, stuffed into shadows, whispering with his underwater voice mumbled clues as to where he'd stashed his son. Elliott listened, but never heard.

Elliott had come in through the back door, leaving his dirty waders in the rear porch. His stomach growled at his wandering mind's promise of hot soup and crackers after his body had been pelted with a hard, warm rain as he fished himself out from yet another muddy ditch, this time minus a fingernail after catching it on a concrete slab whilst dragging himself up an embankment.

The soup was on the boil and Elliott was cleansing the stagnant film from his hands and arms with hot soapy water when the doorbell rang its cheery chime. It was such a happy, alien sound for a house of cold longing.

Elliott dried himself and answered the door. Dr Meadows stood on the porch, his long coat soaked through with the slinging rain, his spectacles peppered with clinging wet diamond droplets. Elliott couldn't see his car parked on the street. He must have walked from the surgery.

'Dr Meadows? What can I do you for?'

'I feel stupid. I've never had to do this.'

'What? Would you like to come in?'

'I can't. I have appointments to keep, I've already cancelled one. I only came to drop this off. It's stupid and horrible and I hate myself being here. But I feel like you should have known either way.' Meadows blinked out rain from his eyes. He removed his glasses, looked at them hopelessly and stuffed them in his pocket.

'What is it?'

Meadows reached into his coat and pulled out a thin, brown card file and handed it to Elliott. He took the file and looked at it, the rain soaking black into its edges.

'What is it Doc?' Elliott asked again.

'I feel horrible. I've sat on this for a week. I've been churning up inside whether to give you this or not.'

'Dr Meadows, just tell me what it is. Please.' Elliott grimaced. He glanced at the file in his now shaking hand, now much more than a sheet of simple stationery, now an ominous portent from some evil reality. Acid burnt out an icy hollow in his stomach, searing through his bowel until he could feel the shrill winds rushing straight through him as if he were a keyhole in a winter gale. Elliott shivered, but not from the cold.

'It won't make a difference. If anything it'll make things worse. But I felt like you should know either way.'

'Meadows, tell me.'

'It's Evan's blood results. They came back. To be sure we'd need to do a biopsy.'

'Biopsy?'

'I'm more or less certain. But it could be lymphoma, it could be leukaemia. I can't tell without further tests. I'm sorry.'

'What are you telling me?'

'Without treatment your son could well die by the end of the year.'

Elliott was silent for a moment. He looked at the folder in his hand as if Meadows had just handed him a grenade with the pin pulled and told him to juggle.

'I . . . I . . . I . . . What can we do?'

'Without Evan? Nothing. It's been eating me up.' Meadows gave a despondent shrug, his face sinking into misery. From the sour expression on his face, this looked like the worst news he'd ever given to a relative, much more than a death sentence, this was a loss of all hope.

'Nothing?'

'Nothing. There are cures, treatments; but you still need the patient.' Meadows shrugged again. 'I thought you should know. This would have happened either way. You shouldn't give up though, if you find him and all is well. There's still time for treatment.'

'Thank you. I'm still looking.' Not *we*. *I'm* still looking. Susannah went to work silently and came home like a ghost through the walls. They only talked about base things such as food, sleep and the weather. She rarely acknowledged his forays into local fields and ditches since his search became less about finding Evan alive and more about finding solid proof of death. Or in the very least a shred of t-shirt fabric or a sighting to flare the hopes he held.

'I know you are. I saw you in Gavin Kennedy's field the other night.'

'I'm not going to give up you know. I can't think of anything else to live for now Evan's gone.'

'Children do that to a man. Good men are always affected by their children. Bad men infect their children.'

Deep inside, Elliott smiled. But nothing came to the surface. The glow had too much darkness to battle through.

Meadows continued. 'If you ever have any bad dreams or anything, anything at all, by all means book an appointment at the surgery. I'll sort you out with something to help you sleep.'

'After a day searching I'm shattered. I drop straight off. No problems there Doc.' Elliott lied. He didn't want the dreams to go away. He treasured every image of his son. No matter how horrific.

Meadows smiled and turned to leave. 'I'll leave you be. I wish you luck.'

'Hey, Doctor Meadows.'

The Doctor stopped, half in the rain. He stepped back under the porch, fresh water pouring from off his nose.

'Yes.'

'Does anybody else know about this?'

'Just the pathologist. But he's not from around here. We send the results away. It's just a number to them.'

'Don't tell anyone. I don't want Susannah to find out. It would finish her. She's fragile enough as it is.'

Meadows stared at Elliott. He didn't nod, or give any indication to what his answer might be. He turned and headed back into the rain, and back down the street.

Elliott headed into the kitchen. He didn't open the file, Meadows's words were enough.

He paused, staring at the file of doom in his hands. Suffering with the power it held over him.

Holding it by the middle, Elliott tore the file in half, then quarters, eighths then numerous ragged squares of confetti. He dumped the remnants in the bin and pushed them down into the rest of the rubbish with his clenched fist.

And that was that.

***

Empty Christmas followed Empty Christmas. They still bought Evan gifts. It would have felt weird if they didn't. Friends and relatives extended invitations but they always refused. They didn't want to tar anyone else with their misery.

Christmas morning they cried. Susannah drank and cried. Elliott stared out the window and cried. After a largely untouched meal of a turkey worthy of cremation and vegetables boiled of all flavour or nutritional value, he continued his now holiday, weekend and evening job of searching abandoned warehouses, hedgerows and anywhere else you'd find a lost little boy. It soon became tradition that finding a body would be apt present to unwrap. Every day without fail, be it wind, rain or snow, Elliott Tather spent his spare time braving the elements. Susannah soon ventured less and less in the search for her son preferring to lose herself in a bottle or two of cheap shiraz or brandy or whatever was on offer at the off licence. Neither could blame the other, and neither questioned the other's new found obsession. It was how they dealt with the dark cathedral filled with loss that their hearts had become.

Another year; then five more. Henry Hollins' obituary appeared in the paper, though neither of them went to the funeral. Ten years passed, forty seasons of blank days hollowed out of any joy they had left. Elliott treated his wife with an anniversary dinner, praying for a sense of celebration and normality. Susannah got smashed on Shiraz, topping it off with whisky from a hipflask stowed in her handbag. This inflamed her to start screaming obscenities at the staff when they brought out a steak that was undercooked. Fearing a scene he fled, flapping a handful of notes at the waiter as they both stumbled out the door.

It didn't matter about their ruined evening, before they even got to the driveway they could see in the flash of warping blue lights that the house had burnt down to a blackened shell. All his time he'd spent out of the house, meant neglect inside the house.

'We're cursed,' Elliott heard his wife mutter, before she collapsed on the baking driveway before their bonfire of a home. The firemen bundled her up in a jacket and carried her over to the fire engine. Elliott stood with her, saying nothing. The dilemma of what to do with Evan's belongings had been answered for them.

A loose roof tile and a damp light fitting was all it took, but by a grim sense of irony, the insurance paid out. Perhaps that was punishment enough, the fact they had the funds to keep on living, to carry on their existence in perpetual anguish.

Despite the cleansing of their lives, the new house was a shell devoid of joy. Friends and family brought round spare furniture and pictures they had of the Tather family in contented times. The photos were thanked for and remained boxed up for the fear of the nostalgia they'd conjure.

Ketchup on Everything

He considered moving town and getting a fresh start. But he was afraid of how Susannah would react. He knew the answer.

What if Evan ever came back here . . . ?

They spent the first week sat catatonic on the cold furniture, staring at the corners of the room as if waiting for an apparition to appear.

Elliott took up shameful, amateurish sketches of his son, scratching graphite onto cartridge paper deep into the cold nights until his fingers locked bent and frozen from his efforts with the pencil.

Susannah took up drinking heavier and deeper into night, to the point where she'd only eat if her devoted husband made her. He had to watch her eat. It was the only way. She became a lurking shadow; a sunken-eyed ghoul that shirked from the morning light, emerging only for afternoon drinks and a few slack mouthfuls of an evening meal. Whilst Elliott continued his subdued existence at work at the insurance brokers, he dreaded what black thoughts coursed through the mind of his wife. Suicide was the obvious answer, though he never broached the subject. Life was dark enough as it was. Besides, he didn't want to feed any wicked inspirations she might be harbouring.

She never blamed him for anything, she was good in that respect. Though he wished she would. He would wish that she'd batter him, or explode on him just to show she was still alive inside, he wanted to see that spark ignite once more. Throw a plate at his head or push him down the stairs, anything to break them both out from this caustic state that rotted them from the inside out.

They couldn't blame anyone else. That was the horrible thing. Even though he'd admitted to himself that he couldn't have done anything different, Elliott still blamed himself. It was too late to learn any lesson. Perhaps others would learn.

Elliott spent his time scouring the papers, missing children became his obsession. As morbid as it was, he hoped to discover a plea from parents about their missing child, vanished in similar circumstances. Just to connect and share grief. Maybe he could help. Maybe.

He collected press clippings, folders become files, files became a filing cabinet, then another. The back bedroom became a vault of other people's misery and lost futures. Floor to ceiling pinned with scraps of newspaper and yellowing photos. He started to contemplate the fact that Evan might have been taken abroad, a theory that daunted him so far as to consider a worldwide search.

He searched for patterns like humans do to understand the nature of the world. The way we look for ghosts in mirrors and photographs, shiver at déjà vu and vainly hope that our bus number, shoe size and birthday will turn up on the lottery one night.

Patterns are a banister for the mind to cope with the fact life is simply a series of horrific events speckled with moments of intense joy

Ketchup on Everything

such as the benefit of marriage, the love of children and the company of good friends. The background is made up of grey tendrils, sometimes it fades black, reaches out and touches you. Then your world is changed forever.

If Elliott wasn't scouring some dark corner of the country with a flashlight and a handful of posters, he was pouring his gaze through files of a books and clippings about unsolved murders and disappearances.

Two cases stuck in his mind.

Eighty-two year old Elizabeth Fields walked away from her bed in the middle night, leaving her nursing home never to be seen again. One resident had looked out of his window had seen a black van parked at the end of the driveway, swearing that Elizabeth had climbed in of her own free will.

Fifty-two year old Malcolm Tinsley's body was found in the burnt out shell of an isolated petrol station in the Scottish highlands. A VHS recording was salvaged from one of the machines that captured the CCTV footage. Playing it back they discovered it had recorded a view of the petrol station forecourt. Customers came and went as the night drew on. The last customer to arrive before the tape cut out had parked just out of view of the camera's gaze, but a reflection in the glass front of the petrol station showed the shape of a black van.

The black van had grown in importance, so Elliott Tather held on to the significance, even though he didn't find any further mentions of it in any more reports of mysterious deaths or disappearances.

He read and marvelled at the fact that close to 300,000 people went missing every year in the UK. Within a year most of them had either returned home or a body was found. There were still up to 20,000 people missing out there at any one time. Some families were left clues, a suicide note or an indication that their loved one didn't want to be found in their new life. But others, like Evan, not a trace was left behind, not giving even the slightest clue as to their disappearance. Nothing.

He was there, and then he was gone as if he'd walked off the face of the planet in a blink.

Abracadabra!

It was truly horrible in its simplicity, and this grim magicians trick consumed the Tathers' world whole.

'Why are you still looking?' Susannah asked during a rare moment of clarity between bottles.

'Because I can't physically, do anything else. I can't stop breathing. I can't stop looking for Evan. Why did you stop?'

Susannah slumped in the armchair as the breath left her in a lilting sigh. She moved her daunting gaze out onto their unloved garden, at the weeds, the tufty green lawn and the waterlogged plant pots the previous owners had left behind

'Because he's dead. I figured that out after the first few weeks. Why waste our lives looking for something that isn't there?'

'That's horrible, Susannah.'

'Life is horrible. The dead pay no mind to the living.'

'So?'

'You're wasting your life. You're better off doing nothing with our empty nest.'

Elliott left it at that. He didn't speak to his wife about their son again.

***

Television became a vague blur in the corner of the room whilst mail, important and otherwise formed a paper patchwork rug by the front door. He stopped shaving, a pair of scissors was implemented when his beard became too long or he caught food in it.

Susannah knocked back a bottle a day, but never seemed drunk. She seemed to function fine on the rare occasions they ventured out in public, never nasty or surly. But at home she became a zombie. They only talked in grunts and nods. They never looked each other in the eye for the fear of contempt they'd see in each other. The last time they even attempted intercourse could be measured in scores of seasons. They'd become strangers bound by the same tragedy, trapped under the same roof because society said they should be there for each other when they didn't even want to exist at all. The only reason Elliott Tather didn't contemplate suicide was because he dreaded what he'd find on the other side, if it existed at all.

The truth.

He wanted to find that out in this world, not the next.

Susannah stayed in bed one week. He was met with curses and thrown cups should he try and help her out of bed. She still came downstairs for nightcaps and eye-openers though. She was dedicated in that way.

He snuck in whilst she snored her way through a guttural slumber. The smell of his wife wasn't of the woman he'd fallen in love with. She'd evolved into a self-made monster, brimming with bile and thin, vicious smiles and sliced out from beneath pits of eyes. This didn't have to be the way, but it was the way she chose.

Her stomach had swollen like a ripe pumpkin, her skin the pallor of dead lemons, whilst veins crept out beneath her clothes like spider legs testing the atmosphere.

How could he let her get like this?

He called an ambulance, and an hour later she was in intensive care. A day later came the certain diagnosis. Cirrhosis. She never woke and passed away two weeks later. He kissed her before they took her away, their first and last peck in years.

Elliott left the hospital and walked and walked and walked until his heels bled into his cheap shoes. By afternoon he found himself outside a Turkish barbers called *Ali Cutz*. He went in and smiled, his grief black eyes creased up as he stared at the stranger emerging from the mirror. The barber was quiet and asked little throughout, only murmuring as he adjusted his client's head slightly as he swept blade and scissor across Elliott's skin with deft precision.

Watching as the tufts of stinking and greying hair fell from his head, they looked alien to him as they were trimmed from his person. Is that how white he'd become? He'd been looking like an antique for too long. He squinted at the face in the mirror. The wrinkles carved out by grief made him look like a map of a mountain gully, each furrow and crinkle was incomparable to the scars of anguish he felt inside. He looked like a beaten corrugated sheet, but the haircut made him feel like he had a little bit of shine left.

Elliott Tather emerged into the cold air, shorn and pink skinned. Reborn. Done with the shackle of his depressive wife, a survival instinct had kicked in, altering him so. Alcoholism was Susannah's way of coping and dealing with the loss of Evan, not his. He wanted action, to piece the world together until he caught even the slightest clue in regards to his son disappearance. That was all. He couldn't ask much more.

Old friends and wary relatives came and went as Susannah was given to the flame. Pats, hugs and tear kissed cheeks became the currency of sorrow. Their words meant nothing. He'd been hanging in there for nearly twenty years, the rope was long frayed but it still held his sanity somehow.

He wanted to scream at them to get looking for his son if they really wanted to help. I don't want food baskets or sympathy cards.

Fuck your lasagne. Fuck your condolence. Stick your offer of a pint up where the sun doesn't shine matey.

In honesty, Elliott was grateful for those that stayed away and offered nothing but their absence.

He kept quiet. Everybody made weak excuses and left.

He was left alone in the world with a jar for a wife.

Her obituary appeared alongside a wedding notice that informed the world that Lilly Vaughn had blissfully become Lilly Greenway.

And that was that.

***

He'd wondered about a headstone. Should he have Evan's name etched alongside Susannah's?

Unlike Evan, he knew Susannah was gone. He'd seen her body before they put her in the coffin, then he watched that coffin burn at nine hundred degrees.

They'd done a sterling job on the makeup. She hadn't looked that good in ages. She'd left him without knowing Evan's fate. He couldn't do that, he wanted an answer to settle his reeling mind. He had to know Evan's fate first, only then he might be pushed to end it with a painkiller and whisky binge, the way Susannah was too cowardly to take, instead of her brave and stupid way of punishing herself gently into oblivion sip by sip.

He had to do something.

Ketchup on Everything

He sold the house and bought a motor home.

Evan hasn't coming back to this town. It had been twenty years.

He quit his job, taking early retirement, where in honesty he reckoned they were glad to be done with his moping around the office. He paid a professional artist to age a picture of Evan twenty years, and then went on the road with what was left of Susannah and five-thousand copies of the new Evan. He went north; posting the picture in post offices, supermarkets, newsagents, petrol stations and anywhere else that would take a copy once he'd stated his case.

Ninety-nine percent agreed warily, others dismissed him as crazy and told him to leave.

He continued his quest diligently as he couldn't do anything else on this earth apart from search for his only son.

It was day two-hundred and five on the road when he pulled into *Sheardown's Steak House and Diner* and ordered a black coffee and a slice of apple and blackberry pie.

The day his life as he knew it would end. He'd get all the answers he'd ever sought and more.

It was the day two weirdly dressed strangers walked into that diner not five minutes after he had, followed by his eight year old son, as young and handsome as the day he'd disappeared.

Ketchup on Everything

Ketchup on Everything

'Is John here?' the tall stranger asked, stifling a dangerous grin. Elliott couldn't see who he was talking to, though he assumed it was Simone.

'Who?' Simone responded, out of sight, though not of mind.

'John? Or are you by yourself?'

'I don't know any John. The chef's called Mark. Are you after the owner?'

'So you're by yourself?'

'Well, yes.'

'We gonna do this in the kitchen?' the female stranger asked from behind the tall man. Her hips buckled slightly, thrusting forward with a minor pulse as if she expected some sexual charge to overtake her. She interrupted the gyration by rubbing her hands into her crotch. Her fingers searched, dug, picked and fiddled at something beneath her dress. Elliott turned his dumb gaze back to the boy who looked uncannily like his son. The likeness was frightening. His son's name whimpered and hung on the edge of his lips. He wanted to cry out his name in joy, race over and embrace him. But a horribly truthful common sense held him back. His son should be in his late twenties by now. His son should be dead. The apparition before him, this stranger was a coincidence. That was all. People have doppelgangers. It happens. But if these strangers walked out of here without him knowing the truth, he'd have to live with the uncertainty for the rest of miserable life. He had to know, but at the same time his mind fought with the reasoning that he'd risk embarrassment at the fault of his mistake. The debate continued as he played out each scenario in the theatre of his mind. Sit down, keep schtum and don't bother the strangers with his problem. He'd carry on with the rest of his life asking a question he'd never find the answer to.

The other scenario wound round his brain, playing in conjunction with the passive movie his mind made. His son was metres away. He was sure that it was him, the likeness was eerie. What if he called out his son's name? Don't make a scene, just say his name and see if he responds. If the strangers take offence or if he's proved wrong, he could just squint slightly and say he'd made an honest mistake.

A saying flared in his mind; *it is better to be quiet and thought a fool, than to open one's mouth and remove all doubt.*

This was wrong. Elliott Tather needed to be proved a fool or risk never being able to sleep again from unknowing.

'Eh . . .' A muttered whisper rose from his throat. He couldn't speak. The frog was his prince, saving his life.

'The kitchen will be good. We'll be out the way in there.' Grinning, the tall stranger removed his Aviators, slipping them neatly into his inside jacket pocket. Elliott watched helplessly as he leaped over the counter and disappeared from view. A scream echoed from the kitchen, followed by a clatter of plates smashing on the tiled floor. Elliott jolted in the booth, the grey hairs on his neck prickling against his collar. A sickly sweat erupted from his skin as the dressy female and his son's doppelganger left the main diner and swaggered into the kitchen with horrifying confidence.

Another pitiful scream burst out from the kitchen. It ended with a gurgle, followed by a girlish snigger.

Who were they?

Psychos emulating the Manson family?

Thieves after filling their greedy pockets from the till?

Drug artists with their minds mashed on plant food and crystal meth?

It didn't matter who they were, they were hurting Simone.

The two scenarios that he'd been considering moments earlier left his mind as his brain switched channels into survival mode and he pondered two new scenarios. Help Simone or get the hell out of the diner.

His frantic gaze flitted around as he searched for an exit. He could either smash his way through a large pane of glass or run for the exit. He had nothing suitable to break the glass with. The seating was fixed and the heaviest item he had to hand was the sugar shaker.

From where he sat, the way he'd come in was the only way out.

Listening with pricked ears, maniacal giggles chattered from the kitchen, interspersed with wet sucking sounds that played over the chorus of *La Bamba*. The energy matched in each soundtrack.

Ketchup on Everything

Elliott sat frozen in his seat for a moment, staring at the empty place beside the counter that the strange trio had left. Unsure of the correct action in such a situation, Elliott did what anybody else did in fear for their life. He armed himself.

He picked up his fork from beside the plate of apple and blackberry pie and instantly felt ridiculous, though a little safer. He had to do something. Inaction was painful. He felt himself slipping down a parabolic curve of certain doom as the less he did and the longer he took to do it, the worse the eventual outcome would be.

The poster of Evan stared back at him. The imagined and the supposed versions of his son looked nothing like each other.

His stomach was a leaky bucket of acid, dripping caustic fluid upon his fraught nerves, fraying their links further. He had to do something, he couldn't hide any longer or he'd lose his mind with not knowing.

Finding momentum within himself, Elliott Tather fought inaction, steeled his jellied knees and squeaked up and out of the seat, the fork tight beneath his white knuckles. He stepped lightly down the centre aisle of the diner, approaching the counter, closer towards the greedy sounds of urgent satisfaction. Dead stars grinned from the walls. From dark ruby lips, Marilyn blew him a probable kiss goodbye and The Duke, squinting, pointed a gun in the direction he was going.

Go get 'em kid!

Elliott reached the counter and peered round into the kitchen dreading the possibilities. He wasn't disappointed. The two strangers and Evan's doppelganger were crouched on the floor beside the grill. Simone's trainer footed legs stuck out from beneath the prone crowd and pointed his way. Her left foot twitched like an inconsistent metronome.

Left, right. Left, left, right. Right, right, right. Left, right, left . . .

The trio of heads bobbed up and down upon Simone's body making wet, hungry sounds. The girl was suckling on the left wrist as if it were a giant, novelty drinking straw, whilst Evan slurped on the right. The tall gentleman was closer to her neck, his mouth making wicked, draining noises upon her jugular.

He hoped she'd just fallen and spilt some wine or beetroot juice, and the strangers were helping her back on her feet.

They must be. They wouldn't . . .

It was strawberry jam, or raspberry jelly. That was all. Simone had slipped.

A pool of blood had gathered around their bent knees like an expanding rug whilst they did whatever they were doing to the waitress.

'Evan?' Someone said. Elliott didn't realise it was him that had spoken until the trio stopped their slurping and looked up at him with eyes cast as black marbles.

They glowered with intense thousand-yard stares that bore through him and the wall behind.

Their mouths were splashed with bright clown red makeup and their teeth bared and slick with half-drunk blood. Each held a twisted grimace, a lion's smirk, a predator's leer, the last thing a meal happens to snap their eyes at before the chase begins and adrenalin floods the veins.

The young boy licked his lips. His hungry animal scowl faded as if in recognition. A sly, half hurt crept across his face. He knew.

'Yummy. Pudding,' the young woman sneered as she turned her body fully towards Elliott. Then she pounced from the pit of slaughter with feline grace, her flat palms caught him in the chest and pushed him back into the booth behind him as if he were as flimsy as a cardboard cut-out. The back of his head caught the plate glass and whirling stars danced through his eyes. He slumped down into the booth with a vinyl squeak. The girl was atop him, her hot copper breath drowning his. He was expecting fangs. But her teeth were normal, they were smaller than what you'd expect to find, so she had lots of them lined up together.

Tight like buttons, Elliott thought before he could think. *They look fuck all like buttons. More like filed down shark's teeth. A Great White in girl's clothing. All the better to gnash you with, my dear.*

They were beautiful teeth. Model dentures that almost looked fake.

His arms contained about as much strength as cooked spaghetti, but somehow he managed to hold her back by gripping onto her shoulders and digging his thumbs in, bracing her driving weight with his elbows against the seat of the booth. Her head craned closer. Blood diluted saliva dripped from her open mouth and onto his face. He contorted his face and held his twisted mouth shut tight, fearing AIDS, hepatitis or whatever blood-maddening disease affected his attacker.

Her teeth snapped shut with a wet clack. The young woman flashed a wide murderer's smile. Maniacal and hungry, unperturbed of the consequences of her actions, she strained closer. She was mad, beyond reason and logic. Elliott would need to find an animal strength from somewhere in order to defeat her.

What the fuck do I do? Elliott's mind reeled, spinning off again as he considered what to do about another life or death situation in the same minute.

What in the fuck do I do?

He noticed the fork still pressed in his hand. To even begin to use it he'd have to let go of her. And that would result in her little teeth around his grey, old neck.

What are you?

He tried to push, she couldn't have weighed much. He should have been able to push her off with ease, but it was her strength that held her down, not her lithe mass. A hook weighs nothing compared to the fish, but the fish still struggles to free itself from the bait.

His arms started to blaze and quake from the effort, willing him to give up and accept his fate. The bright maroon slick teeth gaped closer to kissing his delicate jugular. His wrists bent back and his elbows burned, screaming to stretch. He tightened his face, expecting the impact of gnashing teeth upon his neck.

Am I the bait? Am I food?

'Eloise, stop!'

The bark hollowed out the diner and he felt her jar in fear, freezing as if scorned.

The young woman closed her jaw with all the brevity of a bear trap. Her gory lips remained parted in a bitter contortion. A thick drop of blood crept over her lips. Her tongue darted out to greedily draw it back in, but she missed and it dribbled down upon his chin. Eloise leant in and licked off the spot of blood with a lewd swipe of her tongue. He expected it to be caustic, instead it was overly warm and left him with a pleasant, almost capsicum tingle upon his skin.

She dipped her head and her bright black eyes burned into his fearful glare, colour flushing back into them as some sort of false humanity flooded within. Her eyes were a brilliant jade. She looked upon him as a kept wolf tempted with a titbit by a playful keeper. He was a morsel and nothing more to her.

You'll be mine. Not yet. But you will be mine, he imagined words formed by her hot copper breath.

'Daddy?'

Eloise's grasp on him loosened a little.

'Get off my Daddy!'

Begrudgingly, Eloise did. But first she gave him a playful, lingering tap on the cheek and winked; an apostrophe to her salacious curl of a cruel smile.

***

'Evan?'
'Yes.'
'Is it you?'
'Yes.'
'I . . . I . . . I.'

Any further words failed him. His mouth gaped, giving him the appearance of a mystified, beached fish sucking in dead air wondering as to how he ever came to be on dry land. All the questions he wanted to ask failed to emerge in his mind. Half of his mindset was still on survival mode after the attack on him and Simone. Fear told him to run and save his own skin. But twenty years of wondering kept him cemented to the chequered lino. Twenty years of living without his son, twenty years of harbouring a dark body of insufferable misery. They could have drowned him in rocket fuel and set him on fire and he wouldn't have flinched. He needed answers. If it meant his life, the last twenty years of misery would be solved.

Blood or no blood.

He wanted to hold his son more than anything else, but a grinding survival instinct warned him off. A move at this point would mean death. This had become a game of chess; he had to pick his moves carefully.

Ketchup on Everything

Elliott's eyes flitted back and forth over the three figures. The tall gentleman stepped out from the rear kitchen and into the diner. He wiped his bloody mouth on a dishcloth and slung the sopping rag on the floor with a heavy plop. His eyes were a trusting brown, no black tainted them.

'Ah. It appears we have a situation here,' said the gangly gentleman with a cunning grin. 'Let me introduce myself. I'm Barker.'

He held out his hand towards Elliott and stepped towards him. Elliott buckled back into the booth, fearing the worst. He readied the fork.

'I suppose you're wondering what the hell is going on?' Barker looked at his long fingers as if searching for something wrong with them. He pulled the hand back to his side. Understanding the fear he had caused, he retreated his welcoming gesture. This was no time for pleasant handshakes. Just talk.

'You took my son didn't you?' Elliott asked, soft, and with the patience of a saint. He looked at Evan, then the man now known as Barker. Barker gave a slight nod. But no guilt showed through. He was agreeing with the father before him, nothing more.

'Yes, I'm afraid so. You have a lot to thank me for Mister Tather.'

'Thank you! For what?' Elliott spat, incredulous with a contained rage. He almost laughed. 'You've made the last twenty years of my life a sheer living hell. My wife is dead because of you. You ruined my entire life.'

'Mr Tather, this is a delicate matter . . .' Barker reasoned before Elliott interrupted.

'What have you done to my son?' Beneath the table and out of sight, Elliott tightened his grip on the fork. In his mind he went through the motions of jumping up and out of the booth and jabbing the fork into Barker's long throat before grabbing Evan and running out of the diner and into the moonlit night. He looked at the athletically dangerous Eloise. Her legs were longer than his. He wouldn't make it to the exit, let alone the motor home. He felt the tears well up, threatening to push his eyeballs from their sockets.

'Are you . . . cannibals or something?' Elliott didn't believe the words leaving his lips, but they had to be said. There was no other way to describe what they'd done to Simone. They'd drank her.

'It's an affliction. We can't help it. If we don't feed, we die. It's brutally simple really.'

'You're vampires?' Elliott almost laughed at his own words.

'We don't call it that. That's a fictional term that various media employ to describe our condition.' Barker revealed, 'You could say vampirism is a bastardisation of what we are. Like Werewolves to wolves. The legends that you know today are based on previous sufferers of our affliction. Think of it as a kind of transferrable lactose intolerance, except we need fresh plasma to survive. Sunlight doesn't kill us, but the disease does cause our eyes to be sensitive to sunlight. Our lives are extended somewhat, but are we vampires? No. Not in the traditional sense.'

'We might as well be,' Eloise confessed with a wicked little smile. 'I find it exceedingly hard to keep a job. It's a terrible shame as I used to love a good, hard day at work. I like to sweat.'

'We have to keep moving or our feedings arouse suspicions.'

'You kill people? How long have you been doing this?' Elliott asked, dreading the answer.

'Too long,' Barker sighed, 'we're old money'

Barker turned and stepped back into the kitchen. He looked down at the half-drained body of Simone, at the puddle of blossoming blood. He stood over her, deep in thought, his mind a set of moral scales trying to balance the situation out to the best possible outcome, most likely in his favour.

'She was lonely, she had cervical cancer. She didn't know, but she had it. We can smell it, so can dogs.'

'Surely death is her choice,' Elliott reasoned.

'Death is never your choice; it's selfish if it is. We make it quick, and I think given the choice later on she'd choose our way.'

'What about her family?'

'Husband left her years ago, no boyfriend, kids are all grown up and happy. They'll get a nice payout, so don't worry.'

'But you're killing people.'

Barker bent down and picked up a dessert spoon from the floor and held it up; it had a dark fluid splashed across it. Elliott didn't need to guess twice as to what it was. Barker licked the spoon clean, Eloise giggled.

'We've all got to go at some point. How would you like to go? Riddled with tumours and marinating in your own piss in some overcrowded hospice? Or would you prefer a second of pain as we sever the jugular, feeding into the food chain. You humans are vastly selfish when it comes to dragging out your existence, making those that continue to live around you suffer whilst you rot away before them. End it and save their tears and allow them to get along with their lives. We're all but dust in the end.'

Elliott glanced at Evan. His eyes were wide with fright. Elliott could see that his son wanted to edge forward and embrace him, but another fear held him back.

'Is that the way you see it? I think every moment should be precious, even the hard ones.'

'We don't kill indiscriminately; we pick and choose our meals, we're not psychopaths. Lions, tigers and wolves pick off the weakest members of the herd. We're no different. It's the beauty of nature at work, nothing more.'

It made sick sense; in a moment this psychopath had half convinced him that murder was justified if it was for food. But the fear held high that he might be next.

'Can I go?'

Eloise looked at Barker in the kitchen doorway, then back at Elliott in the booth. She licked her succulent lips again and sent a further shivering tingle down his spine. He had the feeling she was the least reasonable, the dangerous one. At least Barker had shown manners.

'I used to act, a long, long time ago. When you're playing a role, a character, you have to know their thoughts, but at the same time, you don't. You have to forget who you were, you have to forget who you're becoming and discover them as you would your own secrets.'

'Did you act in anything I would have heard of?' Elliott asked, trying to pander to this psycho's sensibilities.

'I did a bit of Shakespeare back in the day if you know what I mean. I loved the crowds at the Globe.'

'Really?'

Barker ignored the question, narrowing his gaze upon Tather's lowly form.

'You can't have your son. He's ours. No matter where you are in life, find something that makes you happy and grab on to it. But don't squeeze, it might pop and disappear forever. You should adopt whilst you have some years left in you.'

'But he's my son.'

'We saved him,' Eloise added, 'he's our boy and we love him.'

'You say the last twenty years of your life have been a misery. Imagine if your son was dead, rotted from the inside out. No good to anyone. That's where you'd be right now. You'd have had to watch him die and wither before your eyes. That's what was wrong with him. You'd have to live with that. That he suffered before you lost him. And you'd still have nothing but the memories of him decaying as his body failed his mind. That would've have been your lasting image of him, a weak and decrepit wretch, wasting away to nothing more than a living skeleton. I took that away from you, nothing more. Evan was dead in your world. I wanted a son. I saved him. If anything you owe me Mister Tather.'

'If that's the truth, then we're equal. I owe you sweet fuck all. I never asked you to take him from me. His life should have been ours to lose, not yours to gain. You're a misery thief. You stole my grief. It wasn't yours to take Barker.'

'Noted, but he'll live a greater life with us. He'll live as long as this world will allow. Cancer cannot touch him, wounds heal, and he'll remain one age. We all will. Look how strong he looks. He's beautiful He'll be preserved. You should treasure this moment knowing he'll always be your son. For as long as forever will allow.'

Elliott considered the trio.

Barker; tall, ghost like, well dressed and well spoken. He seemed to be an errant gentleman from another time. From every horror film he'd ever seen, the legend of Bram Stoker and the roles of Christopher Lee, his mind told him vampire or something of the ilk. The alabaster skinned Eloise was beautiful, her attire suggested tales from the Moulin Rouge and her dirty looking mouth told him that Barker had taken her as an accompaniment to his life, a dress piece and yet a partner in crime. He viewed his son, dressed in black jeans and a smart blue corduroy jacket. He looked well kept and healthy, his hair was longer than when he'd last seen him, but it was kept tidy. They didn't mistreat him from what he could see. The only thing he could trust about these people was that they'd looked after Evan for the past twenty years. He hoped.

'I want my son back,' Elliott said calmly. He looked down at the table, then raised his head to meet Barker's thousand-yard stare. The glaring set of eyes told him the answer already. No.

He leashed his rising anger. It would only bring about his own demise, he reasoned. But still the notion burned at the front of his mind that he would more than happily stamp the smirk off Barker's face for the grief he'd caused.

Elliott pushed himself up and out of the booth. Eloise stepped back, backing off towards the exit, standing between him and freedom. She slipped her arm over Evan's shoulder in a protective mother hen way. He slipped the fork up his sleeve. It was his only defence and he was reluctant to let go of it or let it be known he had it in his possession.

'Will you let me go then?' Elliott asked. He searched both of their eyes for a giving tell, a show of intention, anything.

Elliott watched as Barker looked into Evan's eyes, trying to read his adopted son's mind. Elliott read into Barker's conundrum. If he let him go, he risked exposing his life to the world. If he killed him here and now, he risked losing the respect of his adoptive son. That was if Evan still cared about his biological father. Elliott looked at his son. The black marble had flitted and returned to the more soulful blue. A suggestion of a teardrop pooled up in the corner of the boy's eye, but daren't break through. Maybe he feared showing love for his real father in front of Barker at the risk of repercussions later on. Did he still care about his old man? Did he think about his family? If he didn't, then there wasn't much point in trying to get him back. Either he'd die right here or leave heartbroken. He didn't fancy his chances the way the cards were being dealt. At least he knew.

'I don't think . . .' Barker started.

Elliott interrupted. 'Why don't we let Evan decide? After all, this is about him.' He didn't want to make this move, but he had little else to play with, Evan was his last chance. He put all his chips on him.

Elliott watched as a lump formed heavy in his son's throat. It rose then faded like an alien being hiding within. They concentrated their gaze on each other. Elliott stood up and stepped up from the booth to stand before his son in the aisle. Nobody flinched.

'Evan, your mother is dead. She drank herself to an early grave after you vanished. I spent every waking hour I could looking for you. I never gave up. Even after they told me you might not have long to live, I kept looking. I never gave up. Take a look in the back of the motor home. They're about five boxes of posters. Since your mother died I've been driving round the country putting up posters. I've never given up. And look now, I was right to carry on.'

Evan's eyes searched left and right, looking for the right words. He turned and looked at Barker, letting him see the tears. He looked back at his real father.

'They told me that you didn't want me because I was sick. He told me he could smell it in my blood. They hid me away. They fed me but they wouldn't let me out. I started getting ill. He said he could fix me, but I'd have to eat ketchup if I wanted it to last. If I wanted to live I'd have to live on ketchup. He made me drink his spit. Then they gave me ketchup.'

'Ketchup?' Elliott asked.

Evan turned and pointed towards the kitchen. Towards the still body of Simone.

'Ketchup,' he said. Another world and another language. 'I got better after that. I stopped being sick. I like their ketchup, it's nice. It makes me feel warm. We have it on everything.'

'What have you done to my son?' Elliott croaked, his gaze unfaltering from Evan, digging the fork into his thumb to stop himself from screaming.

'He's alive. You can die knowing he's healthy and being looked after.' Barker turned to the boy. 'Evan, I'm sorry. We need your dad's warm ketchup. The waitress has gone cold now.'

On cue, Eloise left the boy's side and pounced again. It was here Elliott Tather understood everything. They'd been allowed their moment, he'd been granted that much, which was more than he'd expected after the disappearance of his son. Barker had given all he'd dared to risk. Now it was time to die. He'd died once when his son left his life. He'd died a little bit more when Dr Meadows had told him of Evan's illness. He'd died again when Susannah finally lost her battle with the bottle. Now, he figured, here in this diner would be the last time he died.

Elliott didn't have time to retrieve the fork from his sleeve. He ducked down in defence and caught Eloise by her shoulders. Falling back and turning, he distanced himself from her gaping, eager for biting mouth. With the speed she'd hit him, Eloise rushed over him, whilst he fell back onto the diner floor, the breath knocked from his chest. A crash and clatter resonated behind his left ear. Elliott flinched, wincing from being winded, the pain of the impact and the fear of Eloise's next attack.

It never came.

Elliott looked behind him. Eloise lay still, her hairline above her forehead was crumpled in the middle, the skin pinched inward and unnatural. A twisted, still smile fixed on her ruby lips, whilst her eyes stared back at him with a beastly glare. A single line of dark blood trickled from the deep dent in her head. Elliott looked at the shifted condiment counter behind Eloise. His eyes flickered to a clump of frayed hair on the wooden corner. Dark blood acted as an adhesive, gluing the strands in place. Sugar, milk and a jar of mustard had spilt on the floor. Eloise made no effort to get up.

In a narrow distance of fear and death, she was gone, Elliott hoped.

He braced in expectation of her suddenly bursting into flames, just like in the movies. But this wasn't the movies. This was supposed to be real life.

'Eloise . . . my sweet?'

Barker barged past Evan, over the top of Elliott and bent down next to the dead girl to cradle her broken head in his long hands. Her glassy eyes stared back into his without focus or longing. They'd lost their glimmer.

'El?' Barker tapped her still, porcelain face, kissed her cheek and rocked her head side to side. He stroked and caressed, hoping to rouse her. He wept denial in response to this jarring of the norm.

Nothing. It seemed they weren't impervious to injury.

'Eloise? Please darling, wake up. You can't do this to me!' Barker raged. 'Please don't leave me sweetie!'

Still nothing. Elliott felt the danger mounting and felt the heat of Barker's anger before the tall man had even made a move.

'You did this.' Barker seethed, his gaze remaining fixed on the dead girl. With care, he placed her back down on the floor. 'You took her from me. I can't let you go on.'

'I thought you'd already decided that?' Elliott managed to quip. Barker reached across and grabbed Elliott by the throat and pulled him across the floor with frightening ease. With an even pressure from his opposing thumbs he began to crush Elliott's larynx. Elliott sucked in a tortured slip of air. It wasn't enough. It was black air. It did nothing to sate the burning need. He squeaked an airless noise as he tried to seize another pitiful breath. Even less this time. His vision blurred red. The outer edges furred and tingled with a black frame that bled into the cherry gauze over his eyes. His sight was reduced to a backwards telescope of Barker's furious glare as the tall man straddled him like a frothing hound pinching the life out of a caught rabbit.

'If you're not willing to die for what you believe in,' Barker seethed through pink stained teeth, 'then you shouldn't be allowed to live at all.'

There was a brief respite as Barker released his grip. Elliott attempted to claw breath back into his lungs through his broken throat. He wheezed and drowned in the taste of his own copper flavoured fluids. His vision momentarily returned, just in time to see Barker descend upon him, mouth agape.

The pressure to his throat came back, it was sharper this time. A biting crush, that caused an intense spasm to rush through his body as an almost orgasmic flood of energy. He sent messages to his legs to kick out. They ran. His arms fought blindly, clamouring against Barker's face and chest. It was no use. His killer was stronger than him.

An arterial spurt shot up and above them like a boiling geyser. He felt it fall back down and patter across his cheeks with a hot splash.

A wonderful delirium settled over him as his blood pressure dropped and he settled into paralytic shock.

Something crunched, heavenly warmth spread over his neck and chest. He heard a scream that wasn't his.

This is it. Elliott thought. *This is how my search ends. At least I know now . . .*

Light faded, everything faded. Even the pressure on his neck faded.

He shivered.

And that was that.

He opened an eye. Just the one.

Lee Marvin glared off somewhere to his right, Jayne Mansfield pointed pneumatic breasts whilst Johnny Cash gave him the finger. Evan came into view and spat onto his open neck. Elliott gagged and Evan spat again, filling the wound with saliva.

'Try to swallow.'

Without thinking he did. Evan spat again. He swallowed through the hole in his neck.

He felt a compression upon his jugular. His fingers felt and he discovered Evan's lithe fingers holding down a blood soaked towel to the wound.

'I don't know if it'll work.' Evan looked hopefully upon his father. 'It's not really a science anybody understands.' Elliott smiled and placed his hand over his son's and gripped it.

'Bah-karr?' Elliott gurgled.

Evan nodded, indicating behind him. Elliott turned his head a few careful degrees. Barker lay a few feet away facing the floor of the diner, a knife embedded to the hilt in the base of his skull. It was a struggle, but he understood what his son had done. The blade had stopped his brain, the brain had stopped the heart, and Barker had stopped halfway through the act of killing him.

'He once told me that our head and our hearts were our only sudden weakness. Everything else can heal.' Evan lifted the towel and looked at the wound on his father's neck. He narrowed his little eyes in concern; spat on the wound then reapplied it. 'He shouldn't have ever told me.'

'He was lying. We didn't even know you were sick,' Elliott said, surprised at his voice returning. 'I've been looking for you.'

'It wasn't up to me Dad.'

'I know son. I know.' Elliott started to cry, and Evan joined him.

They lay for an hour, both weeping. Evan kept the towel on the wound; Elliott tried to lie still as his tears cleared pink tracks through the blood. If anybody came into the diner they'd probably drop dead from shock at the amount of blood soaking the chequered floor.

After a while Evan looked at the wound. Satisfied, he tossed the bloody rag to one side, and then helped his father to his feet. The boy was strong, his size betraying his strength.

'That should do,' Evan diagnosed. Elliott gently stroked the wound, his skin felt soft, anew even. Akin to a newborn's delicate fontanelle.

'Be careful. Don't touch it too much. You could still break the skin.'

'Oh.'

'We should leave.'

'Okay.' Elliott nodded. His neck was still tender. It felt warm like sunburn. At least he felt something.

'Am I dead?'

'I don't know. I've never asked. I'm guessing we're somewhere in between. Barker described it as an affliction that you learn to live with.' Evan looked around the diner, not at the bodies, but for evidence, any clues to them being there.

'Make sure you don't leave anything behind,' Evan ordered. He knelt next to Barker and retrieved a fat wallet from the dead man's jacket and placed it within his own. Then he stepped into the kitchen out of sight.

Elliott checked the booth he had occupied. He picked up the poster of Future Evan and stuffed it into his jacket pocket, best not to take any chances. The table was clean aside from the half eaten apple and blackberry pie and the cold cup of coffee. He didn't fancy either anymore.

He still held the fork in his hand. He'd never let go of it. He placed it on the table and looked at it, then picked it back up and wiped off his fingerprints with his sleeve.

Just in case.

He returned it neatly next to the slice of pie then followed Evan into the kitchen.

He caught Evan turning on every gas hob. These unlit valves hissed a deadly breath into the kitchen. Elliott watched his son pour cooking oil over Simone's body, then move over to the microwave. He popped open the door and dropped in a small metal saucepan. He closed the door and turned the timer as far as it would go. He picked up another bottle of cooking oil, then with urgency he moved away and ushered his father out of the kitchen with the palm of his outstretched hand. Elliott didn't move.

'Have you done this before?' Elliott asked, looking upon the still, oil and blood- soaked body of Simone. A pang of regret flared within. He couldn't have done anything to help. The damage had already been done before he'd had a chance to save her.

'Once or twice. We've always got to cover our tracks. Sometimes we dump the bodies, sometimes we burn. Anything to hide the wounds. Can we go please? Fire can kill us as well you know. There are still conditions to immortality.'

Elliott didn't budge.

'What are you? You're a monster.'

'I'm your son. And if I'm a monster, you're a monster. Well . . . now you are.'

'Oh.'

'Would you prefer the alternative?' His son said, draining cooking oil over Barker and Eloise.

'No, not now.'

'Can we go?'

Elliott didn't speak. He hurried out the way he came in, his son followed. Bill Haley continued to Rock around the Clock whilst propane filled every square inch of *Sheardown's Steak House and Diner* with its invisible breath.

***

'Drive,' Evan ordered his father. 'Fast.'

Elliott Tather did as he was told, gritting his teeth as they passed the diner, expecting the building to side sweep them across the gravel car park in a burning fireball. It didn't. They made the road, he changed gear and they left the multiple murder scene behind. They passed a blacked out Volkswagen van parked on the verge about fifty feet down from the diner.

He looked across to his son. Evan didn't comment. He didn't need to. The past made sense.

'What now?' Elliot asked.

'What do you mean?'

'What now?'

'Just drive.' His son directed impassively.

'Where to?'

'Just . . . drive.'

A bloom of yellow kissed the dark sky behind them. Elliott caught sight of it in the mirror. He said nothing. He touched his neck; it was still baby-soft. He said nothing.

An hour passed without them saying a syllable. Elliott thought about the life his son had lost. All the toys he left behind; the Ninja Turtles and G.I. Joes he adored playing with so much. His first kiss had been stolen from his lips. Lilly Vaughn should have been Lilly Tather.

Elliott was pulled from this faux nostalgia when Evan spoke, his words thoughtful and cunning. It wasn't the voice of the son he'd known. He'd aged inside, but not out.

'Do you have a change of clothes?'

'Yes.'

'Pull over here and get changed.' Evan pointed to a lay-by ahead. 'And wipe off that blood.'

Elliott did exactly as he was told, dumping the soiled garments in a black plastic refuse sack. Once into fresh, blood-free clothes, he headed back to the front of the motor home and handed his son, the twenty-eight year old boy, one of the posters he'd had made with the artist's interpretation of how he should've looked.

'This is you.'

Evan looked at the poster. He didn't take it. He looked away, back into the night.

'I don't recall much about that day. I remember I was playing in the pool because it was hot. I remember you went inside the house to make lunch. Cheese on toast. Somebody called out to me. But it was inside my head. Then it went black until I awoke at Barker's house.'

'I've found you now. It's okay. They're gone. You're still my little boy.'

'I can't help who I am. That's not me. I'm not a little boy on the inside. I am me. You can't help that. Nobody can. Live with it or die with it. Nothing changes.'

'Did you love them?' Elliott asked.

'I thought I did. They cared for me. Why wouldn't I?'

'Because they kidnapped you.'

'I knew that. I just thought they cared for me more than you and mum.'

'That was never true.'

'I wanted to believe that. But I was afraid to run away. In case they got mad. I had to survive.'

'Are we father and son again? You're not going to leave are you?'

Evan smiled, it was still a boy's smile, Elliott believed it was. He saw Susannah smiling there from the beyond. 'It works better if we're a team.'

Elliott beamed back. His wrinkles creased in a way they'd nearly forgotten.

'There are others out there like us. Not many, but they're all over the world. I've met a few of them.'

'I hope we don't bump into any of them.'

'We shouldn't. Unless they come to find us,' Evan warned.

'What can I expect? Do I change? Tell me what you know.'

'In about three days, it'll hit you. I tried to fight it, but it didn't do any good. In three days you'll need ketchup. We'll have to murder somebody and drink them. We'll need to do that once every few weeks,' Evan said nonchalant and far more casual than required. To see an eight year old be so blasé about the act of murder worried the scales that Elliott found his morals balanced upon. Sure he had his son back, but he'd become a cold-blooded killer. Would it matter? No, he told himself. Elliott had torn his life apart to get his son back. He could justify a blatant and random murder after the levels of Hell he's been through.

'Ketchup? Okay. I can deal with that.' Elliott tried to convince himself that he could kill a complete stranger in order to maintain a relationship with his son.

'I'll show you how.'

'Thank you. What do we do now?'

'Whatever you want... Dad.' Evan grinned, happy to utter that meaningful syllable to the most important person in the world to him.

'Do you fancy going to see a film?'

'I'd like that. We've some catching up to do.'

Elliott ruffled his son's hair and sat back down in the driver's seat. He started the engine and carried on into the night.

After a few miles, Evan spoke up.

'Whatever happened to Lilly Vaughn?'

Elliott smiled.

'She's happy as far as I know. She married Josh.'

Evan smiled this time. 'She married Josh Greenway?'

'Yeah, I saw the announcement myself. Lilly Greenway.'

'Huh, I always thought those two would be a good match.'

'Really?'

'Yeah, they were good friends. I was always felt like I was piggy in the middle with them two.'

Elliott kept quiet. He knew the truth, but Lilly couldn't have waited. She had her own life to live. Hanging onto ghosts won't bring them back. We can mourn and remember, but shouldn't pine and wish our lives away.

He clicked the button for the driver's window, picked up Susannah's urn from the middle seat and tipped it upside down. The grey cloud of his wife fluttered off into the night air, swirling in a plume that followed them for about a mile, before resting on the tarmac, hedges and surrounding fields in an undetectable minute layer.

Susannah was free. He could have waited for the sea or a hilltop vista, but he needed the catharsis there and then.

'Bye mum,' he heard Evan whisper.

His son was back, it wasn't perfect, but it was infinitely better than what he had before.

It wasn't the best, but he was free.

He felt the overly soft flesh on his neck. It had healed, but still, it tingled with a gluey tightening. His son had shown him a miracle. Or maybe it was black magic, voodoo or witchcraft.

He didn't know. Elliott didn't feel any different, nor did he have a sudden, unquenchable bloodlust that required sating with the hot blood of a fresh virgin; maybe in time perhaps.

Elliott looked at his son, who looked out of the window and into the passing furrows of moonlit fields.

When Evan was a bumbling, gurgling, happy little toddler, Elliott remembered the fear and realisation that one day Evan would die. It filled him with such a dread that it brought on black hounds of depression that he struggled to keep at bay when he kissed his beautiful son goodnight. One day, the life of this charming little being would end and all this joy he emitted would cease to be. At every age, he'd wished he could've frozen Evan into what he was at that exact moment, capture it and never let go. Seeing his son discover, learn and grow had been a highlight of his life as it brought him such joy. Was there a greater delight in the world than seeing a child grow up as happy as can be? He couldn't think of one.

Before he'd felt that his life had ended with Evan gone, that the story of his life was over and all the time with his son was lost to tragedy. He had to get through that black cloud of pain to get to where he was today. Now he realised that they'd started a new chapter, maybe even a new book altogether.

He had a lot to catch up with.

But they had time.

They had all the time in world.

Ketchup on Everything

The right of Nathan Robinson to be identified as author of this Work has been asserted by her in accordance with sections 77 and 78 of the Copyright, Designs and Patents Act 1988.

All rights reserved. No part of this publication may be reproduced, stored in retrieval system, copied in any form or by any means, electronic, mechanical, photocopying, recording or otherwise transmitted without written permission from the author. You must not circulate this book in any format. At all. This book is licensed for your personal enjoyment only. This book may not be resold or given away to other people. If you would like to share this book with another person, please purchase an additional copy for each recipient. If you're reading this book and did not purchase it, or it was not purchased for your use only, then please return to Amazon.com and purchase your own damned copy or I'll strike down upon thee with great vengeance and furious anger. Thank you for respecting the hard work of this author. Tell your friends and warn you enemies.

This is a work of fiction. Names, characters, places and incidents either are products of the author's twisted imagination or are used fictitiously. Any resemblance to actual events or locales or persons, living, dead or undead is entirely coincidental and not the authors fault.

If you enjoyed this book (or any book for that matter) please consider leaving a review on Amazon, Goodreads, your local paper, spray painted on a neighbours wall or shaved into the side of a family pet. Word of mouth really is the best advertisement, so pay it forward. Because one day, somebody might say something nice about you.

Nathan Robinson lives in Scunthorpe, England with his darling four year old twin boys, his patient wife/editor and a three legged cat named Dave.

So far he's had numerous short stories published by www.spinetinglers.co.uk, Rainstorm Press, Knight Watch Press, Pseudopod, Static Movement and many more.

He is a regular reviewer for www.snakebitehorror.co.uk, which he loves because he gets free books. He likes free books.

His first novel "Starers" was released by Severed Press to rave reviews. This was followed by his short story collection "Devil Let Me Go." His novella "Ketchup with Everything" is the first publication from Snakebite Horror Publishing.

Follow news, reviews and the author blues at www.facebook.com/NathanRobinsonWrites

Authors Note

When you come up with an idea for such a horrible scenario as what goes down on in "Ketchup on Everything", it's hard to thank anyone for inspiration as it's such a terrible thing to happen to any family. Thankfully, I don't know anyone who has lost a child in such mysterious circumstances. But it happens every day. Children go missing. Most are found. Some aren't, but most cases are rightfully well publicised by the media.

The timeline for the story runs from the early nineties to the present day. The reason for this was I wanted to take away the aid of social media from the characters. Nowadays, crimes are solved, stolen bikes returned to rightful owners and social injustices often righted (sometimes flared by) by social media such as twitter and Facebook. From the beginning, I knew I had to hinder the Tathers' quest in a way modern society could relate to. If you've lost something, where would the first place you'd turn?

Would you ring a friend?

Your parents?

Your children?

Or would you post something on Facebook, tagging your friends and asking the world to share your plight?

Bingo.

When I'd finished "Ketchup on Everything" and was in the process of giving it a final polish, I had a dream I'd lost my son. He ran into a crowd and no matter how fast I pumped my legs, I still fought through the dream treacle and despite my efforts I found it impossible to catch up with him. I glimpsed the top of his hat as he climbed aboard a van with several other children. I ran until I finally caught up with the van and with the urgent clamouring of a prospector digging for gold, I started pulling children out of the back of the van. I found the hat-wearer and it wasn't him. I'd been chasing a wild goose.

The dream moved forward and I was in the front seat of a police van, I even remember their bulky body armour pressing into my face as the driver took corner after corner. We were searching rain swept streets. On and on this went until darkness fell inside my head, then I awoke, got up and wrote these two paragraphs whilst the horror was still fresh.

Thanks

First off, big massive hairy thanks to my amateur editors Marcus Blakeston and Kevin Bufton who are anything but. Good advice for any emerging writers out there, grow a couple more sets of eyes, because even when you think you got everything, you missed something. No matter how many times you read your manuscript.

Raise a glass to my beta-readers Joe Fishburn, Gemma Bryan and Jack Bantry, Paul Johnson and Nanna Elaine. Mwah. The fact that you said you couldn't put it down filled my heart with pure joy and a strange giddiness.

To Dave Vella, for the magic and the parabolic curves

A firm handshake to any new fans I've made since my last thanks. If we've spoken, it's you. The fact that you read and enjoy my order of words is what makes me want to be a better writerer. A wave to my old fans, Kayleigh Marie and Theresa, always and forever.

Goddard; just because he has his heart in horror, it doesn't make him a bad person. Horror is a mirror to society and those who champion it (for the right reasons) should be applauded. Enthusiasm is what keeps the world turning and inventing new ways to do things. We need more people like him.

Big thanks to Kay Vincent for allowing me to "borrow" her design for the front cover. I found her by chance when I Googled the title to see if anybody else had done a similar story, it turns out they do tea towels. For semi-official tea towels, check out www.ketchuponeverything.co.uk .

I'll doth my cap to my Harlequin brothers, who whether they like it or not, are my second family. I'll not name any of the miscreants because some of them are filthy scoundrels. Extra pineapples for Shaun Niland.

Thanks to my parents and to my sister, for never letting me wander too far and keeping an eye on my idiot self for thirty odd years. Good families teach their children how to be good parents.

A hug across mountains, deserts and deep oceans to Matthew and Vijay; brothers who I've found since I started this. Let's not lose each other, yeah?

A gargantuan sloppy kiss to my wife Joanne, who always forgives me for the early mornings and late nights and waking her up when I finally manage to drag my boiling carcass to bed. I don't think she forgives the snoring though.

Hedgehog kisses to Oscar and Henry, who amaze me every day. I wish everybody could have a pair of rambunctious little boys to vanquish all boredom from their lives.

Splatterpunk Zine is a handmade DIY horror fiction zine edited by Jack Bantry. In past issues you'll find new fiction and illustrations by the likes of Jeff Strand, Shane Mckenzie, Dank Henk, JF Gonzalez, Glenn Chadbourne, Robert Ford, Tim Curran, Barry Hoffman, Ryan C Thomas and Nathan Robinson. Accompanying the fiction and art are interviews, book reviews and columns indulging in the world of splatter fiction.
http://splatterpunkzine.wordpress.com/
www.facebook.com/splatterpunkzine

NATHAN ROBINSON

DEVIL LET ME GO

Containing thirteen stories of intrigue and fear, 'Devil Let Me Go' is the first short story collection from emerging new horror talent, Nathan Robinson, author of the acclaimed Starers, published by Severed Press. Each story takes the reader into the dark heart of humanity and beyond.

AVAILABLE NOW IN PAPERBACK
AND ON AMAZON KINDLE

PRAISE FOR DEVIL LET ME GO

"As a short story collection, this is just the right thing for you bedside table- don't be so sure of a good night's sleep though."
THE TERROR TREE

"The darkest stories have snippets of humour and the more overtly comic pieces still have heart. . . Definitely worth a read."
THE BRITISH FANTASY SOCIETY

"These thirteen stories really come together to create an exciting, fast-paced grouping that provides quick, entertaining reads that anyone with an appetite for fear will be sure to enjoy. A fantastic compilation."
THE HORROR PALACE

"Intelligent and poignant . . . you will search long and hard before you find a more suitable selection than this collection. A very pleasant surprise."
READER'S FAVOURITE

"All-in-all, a solid collection. If you're looking for an introduction to his work, it's a great place to start, and if you're already a fan, then you'll find plenty here to enjoy."
BEAUTY IN RUINS

"Outstanding- Thirteen stories that look into the dark heart of human nature. Thirteen stories that will chill you right to the marrow. Don't think twice go and pick up a copy of this collection you won't be disappointed."
GINGER NUTS OF HORROR

They are watching...

Imagine if you found yourself the attention of the entire world.

The dysfunctional Keene family awaken one Saturday to find several strangers and neighbours staring at their home. Events turn more bizarre when more hypnotised strangers arrive, all seemingly transfixed with those within the Keene household. As the ominous crowd gathers and grows larger by the hour the Keene's find themselves under siege in their own home. With hundreds, then thousands of bodies pressing against the walls of their home, a rising body count and grim premonitions plaguing their dreams, the family must work together to discover who or what is controlling the Starers.

PRAISE FOR **STARERS**

"Humorous and thought-provoking, STARERS is a great start from a promising new writer. I'm already looking forward to more!"
The Horror Zine
"The Starers themselves are delightfully creepy in an eerie, suspenseful way reminiscent of the best old-school horror."
Blood Magazine
"Will love survive in the end and lay defeat to the "starers," you must read this novel to find out, it is well worth it tenfold."
Horror Palace
"I want you to appreciate how odd it was for me to, not only finish this book, but get completely lost in it. I had finished this book within twenty-four hours of opening it. The positives are plenty and if you don't mind reading something out of the ordinary, you could find yourself loving this."
The Book Geek
"Dark, creepy, and oh-so-very gory, this is also a book that's often laugh-out-loud funny. Kudos to Robinson for being able to manage that balancing act, and for knowing just when to alleviate some of the tension, without denying the story its unsettling heart. Definitely worth a read."
Beauty in Ruins

Made in the USA
Charleston, SC
28 September 2016